SORRY

ALSO BY

GAIL JONES

The House of Breathing
Fetish Lives
Black Mirror
Sixty Lights
Dreams of Speaking

Gail Jones

SORRY

Europa
editions

Europa Editions
116 East 16th Street
New York, N.Y. 10003
www.europaeditions.com
info@europaeditions.com

Library of Congress Cataloging in Publication Data is available
ISBN 978-1-933372-55-6

Jones, Gail
Sorry

Book design by Emanuele Ragnisco
www.mekkanografici.com

Prepress by Plan.ed – Rome

Printed in the United States of America

CONTENTS

for Veronica Brady

SORRY

PART ONE

ANTIGONUS: . . . thy mother
Appear'd to me last night; for ne'er was dream
So like a waking. To me comes a creature,
Sometimes her head on one side, some another—
I never saw a vessel of like sorrow,
So fill'd and so becoming . . .

The Winter's Tale, III iii

1.

A whisper: sssshh. The thinnest vehicle of breath.
This is a story that can only be told in a whisper.
There is a hush to difficult forms of knowing, an
abashment, a sorrow, an inclination towards silence. My throat
is misshapen with all it now carries. My heart is a sour, indo-
lent fruit. I think the muzzle of time has made me thus, has
deformed my mouth, my voice, my wanting to say. At first
there was just this single image: her dress, the particular blue
of hydrangeas, spattered with the purple of my father's blood.
She rose up from the floor into this lucid figure, unseemly, but
oh! vivacious with gore. I remember I clung to her, that we
were alert and knowing. There might have been a snake in the
house, for all our watchful attention.

"Don't tell them," she said. That was all: *Don't tell them.*

Her eyes held my face, a fleck in watery darkness. Then we
both wept; she washed me away. And when for comfort we
held hands, overlapping, as girls do, in riddled ways, in secret
understandings and unspoken allegiances, the sticky stuff of
my father's life bound us like sisters. Outside, at the screen
door, our kelpie scratched and whimpered, demanding admit-
tance. Mary and I ignored him. The scale and meaning to
things at that moment was obdurately human.

*

How to gather, quietly and honourably, all that is now scattered? How to reanimate the dead as if they were human after all, not symbols, or functions that I must somehow deal with, not flimsy puppet cutouts trimmed to my purpose? When I was born, two years after my parents' marriage, my mother was thirty-eight, my father thirty-six. Neither had expected children; indeed, both were accustomed to self-enclosure and habituated to types of loneliness their partnership did not quite alleviate. I was a mistake, a slightly embarrassing intervention, and knew this melancholy status from earliest childhood. Predictably, both treated me as a smallish adult, arranging a regimen of behaviour, insisting on rules and repression, talking in stern, pedagogical tones. Neither thought it necessary to express affection, nor to offer any physical affirmations of our bond. I was, in consequence, a beseeching child, grumpy, insecure, anxious for their approval, but also wilfully emphatic in ways that I knew would test and annoy them. In the battle between us, there were only losses. If it had not been for the Aboriginal women who raised me, I would never have known what it is like to lie against a breast, to sense skin as a gift, to feel the throb of a low pulse at the base of the neck, to listen, in intimate and sweet propinquity, to air entering and leaving a resting body.

I was born in 1930; part of my childhood was in wartime. My father, who had served as a young captain in the First World War, carried fragments of shrapnel deep in his back and therefore walked with an awkward, halting tilt. He had hated being invalided out of the army—a vague shame attached to his incapacitation—and when war came again he was doubly shamed to be refused a commission. He had become stubborn and mean-spirited, but also intent on proving his manhood. By 1928 he already had the weary eyes of someone disappointed by life, and married my mother, I think, as some obscure, even unnameable, compensation. It was certainly not love; love makes itself manifest, love is a tangible tenderness. It was an assertion against loss, a form of acquisition.

When they met, my father was in his final year reading anthropology at Cambridge; my mother worked as what was then still known as a "lady's companion." My father, Nicholas Keene, had money enough: his father owned four haberdashery stores in London, which he had invited his son to manage. In any case, they promised an independent yearly income. But the sight of mannequins in windows filled Nicholas with dread. He could not have told anyone why he felt swindled by the life his father offered him, and why, when he gazed into the shop windows he would eventually inherit, he felt a dull quiver of morbid trepidation. The garments hanging on lifeless bodies reminded him of the war. He saw before him again the ghastly carnage of 1918, the ruin of mud-caked men, discoloured khaki with death, lying there, gone. His own surprised aliveness had made him feel special, one of the elect, a survivor, a lucky man, even when he was blasted from behind and found his back torn open. He could not have stood behind a counter, dealing with body-shapes of clothing, the arms flapping loose on coat-hangers, the slack torso of any shirt. An anguish he did not recognise made him think of this often—bodies blown to kingdom come, the muck of it, the flesh. He would spend his life negotiating a dangerous contradiction, wanting both to remember and to forget the war.

Nicholas met Stella, my mother, in a shadowy little teashop opposite King's College in Cambridge. As he pushed past a customer, looking sideways for a cosy booth on a freezing day, the tea on Nicholas's tray toppled and splashed someone sitting to his left. My mother called out, sprang to her feet, and with agitated gestures began to whip away the scalding liquid. Apologising, my father bent to wipe her. The stain that spread in her lap was what Stella will later remember: she will describe to her favourite sister, Margaret, how shocking it seemed, how implicitly sexual. Nicholas and Stella sat together, each uncomfortable, but obliged, and realised a tenuous, incipient attraction. Nicholas saw in Stella a plain woman who would not say no if he pursued her, a woman who would no doubt be flattered by his attentions; she saw in him an obscure sign of damage, guessing immediately from the way he moved when he entered the teashop—the little bell above the door made her look up with each entrance—that he had been wounded in the war and was shy and vulnerable. He would be flattered, she thought, if she agreed to walk out with him. In this oscillation of estimations both somehow converged, and agreed, almost without discussion, to meet in the same teashop the following day.

It was not an ardent courtship or an impassioned connection, merely the magnification of an accident and its spreading stain. If there was any romantic grandeur at all, it existed in the looming façade of King's, mauve in the winter light, majestic, austere, that Stella glanced at nervously during their stilted conversations.

On their second meeting she wore her very best hat, a cloche in grey felt adorned by a peacock feather eye, but realised that Nicholas seemed not to notice at all. He was a man who was blankly unmoved by the details of the world; he was given to abstraction in all things, including people. There would be no endearments or simple sweet gestures, no love notes, or flowers or remarks on her looks. Both were given, by long practice, to attitudes of compromise. Both recomposed into the formal shape that would become a marriage, shrank themselves into the half-lives to which they had been subtending.

After his discharge from the army, Nicholas had worked for several years as a clerk in the Bank of England, until he found it intolerable and decided to return to his university studies, interrupted long ago by the declaration of war. But after only a few months studying the law, he changed his course to anthropology. It had the odd grandeur, somehow, of an uncompleted discipline and the challenging allure of frontier encounters.

Having repudiated his father, he decided he must uncover the mystery of what he liked to call "elemental man." His theories on human development and the diversity of cultures were imperial and arrogant. He thought tribal peoples base, unintelligent and equivalent to children, but also that they held in their behaviour and beliefs the origins of sex, aggression and identity. He believed in the British Empire, in its right of governance. The few papers he later wrote, during his time in Western Australia, indicate too that he believed in universalising myths; specificity was less interesting to him than grand design.

According to Margaret, Stella Grant had been an interesting child. The eldest of three sisters (the third was Iris), she developed an early, inexplicable obsession with Shakespeare. Her father was a baker, her mother a housewife; there was nothing in her education or home life that would have predicted a literary infatuation.

She committed to memory a small selection of plays and almost fifty sonnets; she found in Shakespearean language the extravagance and elaboration, a betokening glory, that was lacking in her own much-too-common life.

Stella loved the rumoured universe in which people spoke in rhyming couplets or found intoxicant sentences and daring expressions. Apart from the stories themselves—inevitably of murderous or magical love—there was this flaunted language, this rude excess. So much existed in the declaimed desires and fates of others, in the magnitude of what speeches might form and express. In a life in which so much was hidden or unsaid, in which pass the butter was the only dinner-time utterance (since her father, when he was there, believed children should be seen-and-not-heard), in a life governed by complaint, boredom and tedious attentions to domestic niceties, this world was utterly hers; she was clad in private satisfactions. And although Stella did not believe, like Hamlet, that there was "a divinity that shapes our ends," she admired his questioning misery and made it her own.

At night, after lights-off, she lay in bed, softly reciting. Margaret remembers this was the chant she and Iris fell asleep to. She remembers her sister's whispery sibilance and the bewildering quality of words and ideas she did not yet understand. Her voice, Margaret would say, still returns to me sometimes; it returns only in the darkness, just before sleeping. Only in the darkness, my sister, Stella.

When Stella left school she worked for a time in a confectionery store, wreathed by the scent of sugar she would come to find cloying and repulsive. She served spotty brats and their indulgent mothers, and each time she tipped a mound of bull's-eyes or twisted a paper bag, she felt diminished. She hated her meaningless life, marked out by pennies' worth of boiled sweets, gaudily striped, and the click of purses opened and closed, and the counting of small copper change, and the daily, infuriating, condescension.

Stella learned of a position as a lady's companion, and found that it included the task of reading aloud. She decided that this would be a new captivity she might better endure. The lady, a Mrs. Whiticombe, was a widow from the Great War who, as it happened, did not require much companionship. Stella was at liberty for at least half the day and developed over time a moony passivity, a sort of easy, wandering, dreamy suspension. She lost sight of her own life as a separate thing, and one day woke to discover she had been a "companion" for almost twenty years and that the old woman before her, now in her eighties, was withering away.

When she met Nicholas Keene in the teashop Stella saw her escape, and Mrs. Whiticombe obligingly died three weeks after the incident of spilled tea. Nothing was left to Stella in Mrs.

Whiticombe's will. Despite her years of service this seemed somehow explicable; she had more or less, after all, ceased to exist. There was a convenience, therefore, on both sides in her marriage, although Australia was not mentioned, not even once, and she would never forgive Nicholas his presumption in dragging her, unconsulted, to the dark other-side of the planet.

At their wedding in the registry office Nicholas's father cried. He removed his spectacles and dabbed his eyes in a manner those assembled found embarrassing. Of his three sons this was the only one still alive, and he could finally imagine grandchildren and the continuation of his name, the gold signs of "Keene & Sons" granted perpetuity. Stella's parents were also there, as well as her sisters, Margaret's husband and her daughter and two sons. Margaret said that Nicholas did not once encircle her sister's waist, and that both groom and bride appeared throughout to be having second thoughts.

Stella wore a sprig of cloth violets pinned to her collar; she fiddled restlessly, she appeared preoccupied. Mr. Keene senior arranged a fancy supper at the local hotel (roast pork and beer, with afterwards a rich plum trifle); but he was the only one, the family decided, who thoroughly enjoyed himself.

It was a grey, gloomy day, with the threat of rain. There was no dancing and Nicholas drank too much. Among the practical wedding gifts—pots and pans, a Swiss clock, a set of Irish linen—lay, neatly folded, a Spanish shawl. Margaret had ordered it from Cadiz for her sister. This shawl, black and tasselled and embroidered with looped patterns of scarlet poppies, became for Stella the sad emblem of all her lost dreams, of all that was unShakespearean about her life.

This Spanish shawl is the only garment of my mother's I still possess. When I wear it I think of her, all those years ago, a brand-new bride, peering ahead at the dim unknowable future, still untouched by my father's embrace and still so uncertain. I wrap myself in what I imagine to be her unspoken misgivings, her sense of fatalism, her staunch opinions. The feel of it soothes me. It is soft and enveloping as memory. And now, a lifetime later, this shawl returns the shape of Stella's shoulders and the particular inclination of her head. From the dark and backward abysm of time, a lift of the chin and a profile against the light.

*

I developed my stutter at ten, after my father's death. Until then I had been fluent as any child, a chatterer, in fact, a blithely self-satisfied speaker. But suddenly I began to see words before my voice could claim them; they preceded me like a vision. Seeing the saying made it impossible. In my mouth syllables cracked open and shattered, my tongue became a heavy, resistant thing, words disassociated, halted and stuck. It was easier, I found, if I spoke at the level of a whisper, but even then I would sometimes see the words dumbly accumulate; they would roll in my head, like mist, like water, then emerge blurted and plosive, like something unstoppered.

Because of this affliction I spoke less and less. I began silently to read, finding that words in books, played in my head, held their rhythmic integrity. Others began to consider me a secretive child, or felt mild compassion, mistaking my silence for grief. My mother despaired. She was in a foreign country, without the wherewithal to return home. And now, as she put it, she was a widow, alone, and burdened with a stubborn, idiot child. She raged and scolded. She told me to pull myself together. But somehow, in language at least, I remained pulled apart. I had not until then thought myself so made up by words. I had not known how fundamentally a child might be recreated.

*

Nicholas chose Australia for his field work because it appealed to his sense of the insane: what intelligent Englishman would go willingly to Australia? A black continent, certainly, and full of intractable mysteries. Perhaps Nicholas also wished to punish his pale insipid wife, to drag her away from her sisters, to make her more dependent. Marriage had not been what he had expected; frustration and regret were already its features. Nicholas did not know that he would stay for over ten years, and that he would die there, aged forty-six, in a warm pool of his own blood, smelling dirt in his nostrils, listening to flies hover on desert wind, thinking in his extremity of everything and anything, anything that is to say, but England.

The country to which Nicholas and Stella came in 1930 was alien and indecipherable. There was an economic depression, a fear of communists, a secessionist movement rising in the west. There was a shabby genteel aristocracy, gold millionaires, indigent labourers and an isolationist attitude. Anthropology must have seemed to many a purely useless pursuit.

Nicholas had a meeting in Perth with the Chief Protector of Aborigines, and was told that his field-work projects would be useful in the governance of the natives. Aboriginal people were susceptible to the misguided influence of Reds and Foreigners and likely to be persuaded to sedition by God-bothering Missionaries. They needed to be watched, assessed. There had been "disturbances," the Protector said. There had been casualties. Something hush-hush, apparently. Something unmentionable. Without enquiring what he meant, Nicholas felt assured of the importance of his work, knowing he would report back to agencies of the State.

In Perth, Nicholas and Stella boarded a merchant ship heading up the west coast. Nicholas possessed government papers, which he waved authoritatively, and the crew eyed him with suspicion and mocked his snooty accent. Nicholas watched as they yarned and smoked hand-rolled cigarettes, their manner collective, wry and self-assured; they swore, made crude jokes; they were their own community. He tried to join in, but was not admitted. Since he could not bear retreating to the claustrophobic cabin where Stella was ensconced, defiantly reading Shakespeare, he befriended the captain, another Englishman, as it happened, with a handlebar moustache not unlike Kitchener's, whom he regarded as his only possible companion. Captain Smith gave Nicholas the benefit of his semi-local knowledge. The Aborigine, he said, like all primitive peoples, had a tendency to expire on contact with a superior race. It was the sad duty of Civilised Man to raise or erase the lesser humans, to enable the March of Progress and the Completion of God's Plan. He confirmed that knowledge of how the black buggers thought would be useful in their management and control.

Nicholas watched the captain extract a thread of tobacco from the tip of his tongue and flick it away. He admired this man, a man of action. The world, Nicholas thought, was built by men like Captain Smith.

When he returned to the cabin, Stella was propped on the bunk, reading *The Tempest*. She wanted them drowned. She told him so. Something in their marriage had temporarily capsized her passivity. With wild eyes she stared up from under crumpled sheets and declared in a wicked tease: "*I'll warrant him for drowning, though the ship were no stronger than a nutshell, and leaky as an unstanched wench.*" The cabin smelled of Epsom salts and potions against seasickness. Nicholas turned away. "*We split, we split!*" she cried out after him. Her voice was frayed and mildly hysterical. The vessel of their marriage was already sundered. The ocean around them heaved and roiled, and Nicholas, momentarily nauseous, felt like a child, afraid. His hand grasped the cold metal railing that led him back up the iron stairs, away from his wife and her fierce, lunatic quotations.

In Australia, he knew, he would be a better man, more substantial and more determined. His wife would settle down. She would be well-behaved. He would find again the young man he was when his brothers were alive, full of potential, confident, sure of each step he took towards the future. The bodies of his brothers were rotted in Flanders, forever foreign, but here he was, in a new world, on a new adventure, bent on discovering the why and the wherefore of primitive man. It would be no explanation, but at least a kind of purpose.

2.

It is difficult now to know what words might truly report them. Parents are recessed within us, in memory, in feeling, in ways we sometimes know best at faltering, precarious moments. A confident description is no guard against the discrepancies they hold for us. There is fond reminiscence and fickle recall; there is the freight of unsaid grievances and encumbering sorrows; there is stupefied infantilism and the persistence of their power. And more, perhaps, there is our faint speculation as to their indwelling lives: what lusts and frustrations, what cruelties and kindnesses, what dreams avowed, enacted or disavowed. We are puzzle-headed when we think of them. We are always subordinate. The cartoon they make for us can never be adequately drawn. In any case, some elusive dimension attaches to the imagining of lives that existed before we did, and to those, of course, no longer still alive. Telling stories, even in a whisper, carries this insufficiency.

I believe that in Australia, my father, Nicholas, felt once again heroic. He was a frontiersman, white, filled with colonial aspiration. When he and Stella disembarked in Broome, in the remote north-west, he sensed immediately the promise and seduction of adventure; but his wife, looking backwards, sensed vacancy and desolation. The brassy light enveloped them, stunning in its brightness; there were wondrous high skies and broad horizons, so that Nicholas felt expanded, as if on a mission. Stella, on the other hand, squinted in a rim of shadow beneath her broad linen bonnet, smoothed the front of her stiff poplin skirt, and believed that her life, just begun, had already ended. She developed a tough fury that she would exhibit for the rest of her life, so that it predominated even when she might have found reasons to be happy.

A trader from the ship drove them in a rattly Ford jalopy from the jetty to town. This was largely an Asian and Aboriginal town, built around the pearling and cattle industries. There were Japanese and Malay pearl divers, Chinese tradesmen, Aboriginal stock-workers, a tiny white community of owners and managers. Corrugated iron shacks lined the red gravel roads, many of them rusted, aslant, looking drunkenly derelict; there were boab trees, mudflats, mangy wandering dogs. Pearling luggers, caught by the receding tide, listed in despondent formations beyond mangrove swamps; the sea was visible, a strip of shine at a muddy distance. In town, small groups of Aboriginal people sat talking in peaceful clusters, or lounged in doorways, or on narrow verandas. It was a slow town, calm. There was a serene equanimity in the way the locals moved, in the hush of their talk, in the gestures of solicitude by which greetings were made and tasks were performed.

Stella peered from the cabin of the truck and could not understand what she was seeing. So many coloured people. So many foreign faces. For her this was a place of utter barbarity, and she had yet to learn that this was not their final destination. Nicholas had arranged a stay at a cattle station in the scrubland of spinifex and rocky outcrops, twenty miles southwest, so that he might be within scholarly proximity of his chosen Aboriginal tribe. Papers from the Chief Protector of Aborigines—who owned, in a sense, an entire people—instructed Nicholas on a location, and indeed the terms of his project. Only later did he guess he was being cast aside, sent where he might be most useless and forgotten.

They arrived at a modest whitewashed building, wooden-panelled and set on low stilts, called, somewhat grandly, the

Continental Hotel. That first night, lying together beneath the high flimsy cone of a mosquito net, Nicholas tried to reason with his wife, but ended up hitting her. Stella instantly quietened. The bed they shared, enclosed against the tropical night and its streams of buzzing life, was sweltering and forlorn. It represented the world made brutal, another entrapment. Stella wept before she performed her wifely duty. Later, sticky with sweat and sexual fluids, aware of the smarting pain that had overtaken her face, she woke in the middle of the night, released herself from the net, and sat alone, on a hard chair, softly reciting sonnets.

> As if by some instinct the wretch did know
> His rider loved not speed, being made from thee:
> The bloody spur cannot provoke him on
> That sometimes anger thrust into his hide,
> Which heavily he answers with a groan
> More sharp to me than spurring to his side;
> For that same groan doth put this in my mind:
> My grief lies onward, my joy behind.

In her own ears her voice sounded plaintive and full of loss. It sounded shabby, as if she had suddenly aged, become one of the women she had seen in London living beneath shadowy bridges, with their lives in string bags and their wits asunder. It made no sense.

When the recitation offered no consolation, Stella wrote a letter by faint lamplight to her sister Margaret, telling her in lurid detail all that had happened. There was relief, after all, in silent words. In her *own* words, in those that fell in a cursive stream from her own inky pen. The nocturnal world, fractional and slow, continued around her, wheeling towards dawn. Powdery grey moths hurled against the window screens. On the ceiling small lizards, the colour of her skin, clicked and scampered, their hand-shapes clinging. Stella watched them dispassionately. She resigned herself, that night, to gigantic unhappiness, the kind that novelists don't write of, the kind that doesn't kill, but preserves monotonously some empty reg ister of experience, so that one waits, and waits, and waits, and waits, until whatever bitter end might mercifully present itself.

At dawn Stella roused. She opened the door and pushed into a world dank and steamy with overnight rain. Unfamiliar flowers and raucous birdsong greeted her. It was like waking into a dream she did not understand. In the hotel kitchen, a wooden shed out the back flooding with vaporous new light, she met a kindly black woman who made her a cup of tea. She watched the woman at her morning ministrations—tending the fire in the stove, shifting pots and kettles, laying out teacups and spoons in symmetry on a tray—and understood that there are forms of order that might release one from meaning, ordinary tasks that might fill up an unfair life. She did not deem it necessary to talk to this woman; Stella was too disconsolate to express her own humanity. So she sat, tired now, bloodshot and hollowed by her wakeful night, and for some reason remembered Mrs. Whiticombe's old-woman's hands, ropy and frail, spotted like old leaves on the verge of disintegration, resting on a pink candlewick bedspread at the moment of her death.

*

The wind in the scrubland was sear and soprano. It burned and sang. When it was high, it hoisted eddies of umber dirt, so that the air filled with grit and was choking and dry. There were the swollen forms of spirals and belly shapes moving across the land; Stella found them eerie and preternatural. She learned to bring in the washing so that it would not be coated with dirt, and to close the doors and the shutters until the dust storms departed. She learned, most of all, to seal herself in, to find what solace might lie in self-erasure.

Their lodgings at the cattle station were away from the main house, a small shack that had belonged to the stock manager before he suddenly left. When Mr. Trevor, the station owner, first opened the door, Stella had seen nothing at all that could claim her affection. There was a combined kitchen-sitting room, ringed with faded yellow curtains, containing two upright wooden chairs pushed beneath a severe table; and a single bedroom, in which stood a sagging bed and a wardrobe, anomalously elegant, from another place and era. Disturbed by the sudden scrape of the door, a brown snake had slid out into the light and headed swerving through the doorway towards the long pale grass. Stella squealed as it passed her.

"Better get used to it, luv," Mr. Trevor said. He was unconcerned. He watched the snake depart and then spat on the ground, a hearty gob, as it disappeared.

Nicholas marched forward to disguise his fear. He too was rather alarmed by what he had arrived at, the austerity of it all, the danger of remoteness, this slantwise light that revealed the cruel hardness of things. In the pit of his stomach he felt a seizure, a wrench.

"Good-oh!" he declared, and Mr. Trevor, his hands on his hips, stockman's hat tilted away from his sweaty forehead, bent forward and let out a derisive snort.

When Nicholas pulled back the yellow curtains he saw in the distance a clump of acacia, and beneath it, in sparse shade, resting in the groove of a dry creek-bed, a family group of about ten or twelve people. They would be the subjects, or rather, the objects, of his research. They looked, he thought, rather mundane, not noble savages or extraordinary specimens of humanity. They wore cast-off clothes, mostly filthy and shredded, and had matted hair and looks of drear resignation. They roasted a lizard—one he would later know as goanna—

in the ashes of a fire, and passed a canvas water bag between them, each taking a swig. He had read of this communalism, but found the sight of it disturbed him—so much bodily correspondence, so much touch and exchange. In a purely impulsive gesture Nicholas waved from the window, but no one saw him. The family continued their meal as if he did not exist.

That night, tossing fitfully on a lumpy horsehair mattress, Nicholas dreamed he left the house through the yellow-curtained window (as one is magically able, floating in dreams) and joined the Aboriginal family around the fire. He sat in the dirt and shared their meal. The meat was oily and hot, and he had difficulty chewing it. Sinewy muscle and foul-tasting flesh filled up the chamber of his mouth, pushing it outwards so that his face distorted. Nicholas felt himself gag, and then began to vomit. He soiled his own trousers and was reduced, since he could not find the bag of water, to wiping away the mess with his two bare hands. An old man laughed at him, exactly as Mr. Trevor had done, with the same tone of superiority, and the same mocking dismissal.

And that night, for no reason, Stella dreamed that there was snow falling softly in the desert. As if beneath a plastic dome, or confined in the more expensive glass ornaments, she saw the slow descent of flakes, a little too large, and petal-like. In her dream she opened the front door and walked across its threshold, but did not feel the chill of snowflakes settling on her skin; they seemed to evaporate before they touched her. The place looked the same—barren, Australia, the light was glaring orange and the sky extensive—but held suspended this dissolving, impossible drift. In her new country Stella would dream this dream many times. It was always the same. There was always the stepping through a doorway, a sense of keen disconnection, of indefinable loss, and then of the air filled with delicate, illogical presences. She loved to tell it; her snow dream. She told it to anybody who would listen. She must have told me her snow dream ten or twenty times.

*

My own dreams of my parents are always unpredictable. I used to dream that I bent above my father's face and tried to prise open his stiffened dead eyelids, thinking to resurrect him. Then Mary would appear, and she would take me by the hand, and we would leave him lying where he fell, in mortal rest. Or I dreamed I opened the door to our shack, and there he was, a flash of light from his old-fashioned horn-rimmed spectacles signalling his arrival. He stood there, hitting his hat to shake away raindrops.

"You're back," I said, guilty I'd not missed him, surprised by the rain. He was alive or dead; I was never quite sure. He was indeterminate.

Of my mother, who lived until she was almost sixty-eight, there are many, and many more complicated, scenarios. Her animosity towards me I deflected in dreams and tried, by means of my own poetics, to convert it to the friendship we might ideally have had. She was often smaller in dreams, and not so formidable. Our kelpie, Horatio, was usually there, and sometimes we were simply walking, side by side, but for some reason unable to see each other. We looked in parallel, and talked of commonplace things, of the weather, snakes, the people we knew. Once she fell into a hole in the earth but I could not quite reach her and when I peered into the hole, an almost perfect cylinder, I saw only two dull lights that might have been her eyes and I had to leave her there, languishing, calling out my name.

In my dreams I still sometimes stutter, even though, at four-teen, I had been trained to overcome it, or at least to disguise my remnant halting. The images are fluent, but the language is difficult. My mouth seizes, convulses, forgets its easy applica-tions. And in my dreams my father and mother do not appear together: it is as though I have always known they never quite met—never met, that is to say, as lovers do, with intermingling and exchange, and with lips corresponding.

The afterlife I give them in dreams spooks me a little, but no more, I suppose, than this speculating testament. However, it seems still improper to dream of the dead. There is no satisfaction in their return, only metaphysical disturbance, the fake conjunctions that pretend somehow to be meaningful, now, only now, that there can be no repair.

*

Mrs. Trevor was a large, hefty woman, capable and determined. It was she who told Stella outright of her pregnancy, and recommended ginger crackers and barley water for morning sickness. A mother of five, she considered the experience of maternity unexceptional and better dealt with by robust and practical action than what she here perceived—retreat and denial. In Stella Keene she saw a woman afraid of life, and made it her task firmly to re-educate her. Of her five sons, two were out droving, somewhere to the north, and two were at the Anglican boarding school in Perth. The youngest, Billy, a simpleton, was still a child at home. She missed her older sons but found company in the domestic help in the house. There was a cook and two girls—"station blacks," the whites called them—each sent by the Protector of Aborigines to learn the crafts of cooking and cleaning. These were "half-caste" girls, in need of assimilation. Mrs. Trevor—Vera—thought it her duty to civilise them, and to teach them good behaviour and habits of tidiness, to induct them into submission and quiet compliance. To Stella each of the girls, Martha, the cook, and Sal and Daff, all looked desperately unhappy. They wore loose floral-patterned frocks, all made of the same cheap material. They stood leaning together, conspiratorially, as if wishing to merge into one floral being that would conquer Vera Trevor.

For both Stella and Nicholas, the pregnancy was proof they had entered a land of unreason and disparity. It shamed them both, but they were not sure why. Why should there be this surplus, when they had so little to give to each other? Why this person-sculpting, when they were both so concluded? Nicholas ordered a medicine to make it go away, but when the parcel finally arrived the cap had loosened, so that what they received was an empty bottle in a wrapping of brown paper, inked by pharmaceutical spillage. And as Stella grew larger, Vera Trevor's sincerity took over. She made it more difficult for Stella and Nicholas to tell themselves, each night, that nothing would eventuate, that malformation would kill it, that it would never develop, that it would likely expire at an untimely birthing.

The couple watched the signs of gestation with a sense of revulsion. Nicholas found his wife's bulbous body too intrusively visible, and Stella felt dull, overtaken, a heavy conspiracy of matter. They fell into habitual silence. They did not talk to each other. Their shared misgivings remained unspoken.

Nicholas meanwhile resolutely went about his work. Into his head flew the abstract nouns of his book-learning; diffusionism, mythology, ethnological genealogy. Yet his categories seemed irrelevantly abstruse when faced with these shy black people, who would make no eye contact but had a good sense of humour, who seemed—surprisingly to him—intelligent and quick-witted, and were at home sitting on the earth and hunting and gathering its produce. A stockman from the station, Willie, served as a translator. Nicholas had not expected to find these people engaging. At the same time, it was a confronting physicality that at first repulsed him. He found the shiny black bodies altogether strange. Many of the men had cicatrices inscribed on their chests and upper arms, raised welts that signified initiation or high degree; many of the women had pendulous breasts, exposed, that he could not fail to stare at. The children were unclean, he thought, with glistening mucus beneath their noses, and seeds and dirt, sometimes in clumps, studding their oily matted hair. Sitting cross-legged was difficult, and he was always overdressed in the violent heat. There were flies and unidentifiable biting creatures. It was uncomfortable work. Eventually Nicholas ordered a folding table and canvas chair from Broome, and took these with him into the "field," much to the amusement of the community of his research.

3.

It was the wet season when Stella heaved me out, wetter than the air, smeared with her inside life of fluids and juices, yowling, irascible. Vera Trevor yanked me lifewards and cooed almost immediately—"a daughter!"—at what Stella thought was a bloody mess and utterly unlovely. Rain was beating on the iron roof so that there was a density and amplification to the world of substances; plashing, drip-drip, the cascade of waterfalls and spouts, frog-life, scampering things, clay earth subsiding into overflowing sluices and channels. Thunder boomed in the sky. The humid heat was unbearable. Nicholas came in from the leaking veranda, where he had been pretending to read, and saw his wife flushed and prostrate, resembling an animal. He had wanted a son. If he was to have a child, it had to be a son. He thanked Mrs. Trevor for her dedicated service and was annoyed when he discovered that she did not want to leave. There were woman things, she claimed, yet to be imparted. Feeding. Caring. The correct procedure with babies. In an enamel dish, at the end of the bed, Nicholas saw the purple placenta, netted in grey veins, trailing its twisted umbilical cord. It was a meaty, offensive, unaccountable thing. He felt a surge of illness in his guts, and looked away.

The baby was producing mustard shit and had a maroon complexion. It cried at a volume too large for its size, and bunched its face like an overripe tropical melon. Mrs. Trevor said this was normal; she told Nicholas not to worry. He was not in fact worried. He wished privately—although he knew it was a sin—that the newborn baby would not survive. In the nights of sleeplessness that followed, Nicholas felt an evil, irrepressible resentment; he was undone by this advent, he was made base and self-interested. Fatherhood ought to have been a kind of ennobling, but for Nicholas the experience was above all of anxiety, and of the collapse of his work-life and some inner defilement. Before the first week was out, Mr. Trevor—"call me Freddie"—had offered to take Nicholas into the bush, so that the women could get on with their business, he said.

"Like the blackfellas," he added. "Some kinda secret business."

He touched his nose, like a music hall comedian. Nicholas gratefully accepted the invitation to flee. When he said goodbye to his wife she barely acknowledged him; her face was averted, turned to the damp wall. Nicholas could smell the stale tang of women's blood hanging in the air. There was a whiff too of the fecal, of something raw and unsanitary, and of cloths and sponges turning in the heavy wet atmosphere to mould. He wondered what he had seen in her, those days in the Cambridge teashop, when he suddenly decided, there and then, to take a bride. He wondered how he could have believed in any prospect together.

These days it would be named—post-natal depression— but then Vera Trevor simply noted that Stella was "down," that she showed no interest in her baby and was uncommunicative. Stella spent hours of each day remaining in bed, detached into a feeble, drifting state, futureless and sad. She heard her irrefutable baby wail with hunger, but could not be persuaded to offer her breast. She felt absent, inessential. Birthing had scooped her out.

When Mrs. Trevor asked how she felt, an innocent enough enquiry, Stella replied: *"You do me wrong to take me out o' the grave . . ."*

She sounded plumb crazy, Vera Trevor said later. Mad as a cut snake; mad as a blimmen meat-axe.

Mrs. Trevor found a wet nurse among the station blacks, and had her sleep with her own infant, a boy, on the floor of the shack; meanwhile Sal and Daff were assigned mothering duties between them. In her lonesome state, wrecked by her own body, Stella was aware of the little community constituted around her; the three women (the wet nurse was Jukuna, a Walmajarri woman from the desert) and two babies, one black and one white, and the circulation of soft voices in a language she did not understand. Sometimes, in a haze of delirium, she thought it sounded Shakespearean, so full was it of convolution, evocation and rhyme. Something that might have been an ampersand, if it had a sound, repeated again and again, so that what she heard were connections and collusions affirmed: a bracelet of propositions, perhaps, or an extra logic of meanings, from which she was excluded. In words—she knew it— there were these revealed affiliations, these sensible families. In words, body-forgetting, there could be intelligible experience, not this crude engulfment and drowsy clouds of unknowing.

It was two weeks before Stella was moved to give the baby a name. "Perdita," she called it, without even hesitating. Vera Trevor said politely it was a pretty name, but she had never heard of it and thought perhaps it was posh English, or an obscure, archaic family inheritance. Stella was questioned, later on, when she had returned from the land of her illness, and explained that Perdita was the daughter of a dead woman, that Perdita was a character, a princess, from a famous English play.

Mrs. Trevor had arranged for Stella Keene to be sent to the hospital in Broome, "for a rest," she said. The baby meanwhile flourished in black arms, which found and embraced her. Perdita grew chubby, contented and well.

*

I do not remember when my mother first told me this story. I was perhaps five or six, already aware of the estrangement between my parents and of some sullen accommodation that enabled them to stay together. Small children intuit, heretically, the most hidden understandings. In the involving machine of parents' behaviour, their words and their silence, their actions and inactions, the child learns what is valued, and what counts for nothing. They didn't count to each other, my parents. And they barely counted me. I was a foreign coin they possessed, a worthless shape.

Stella told me that in the Shakespearean play called *The Winter's Tale*, there was a king, Leontes of Sicilia, as powerful as he was unjust. In a jealous rage he accused his pregnant wife, Hermione, of dreadful crimes, and though she, and everyone else, attested her innocence, the king would not listen and had her imprisoned. In prison Hermione gave birth to a daughter, Perdita, and the king ordered his courtier, Antigonus, to dispose of the infant. But Antigonus was good-hearted and abandoned the baby, as it happens, on the sea coast of Bohemia, whereafter he was immediately eaten by a bear. ("Exit, pursued by a bear," read the famously silly line. I hated this bizarrely particular detail.) Perdita was found, and raised by friendly shepherds. Sixteen years passed. The king had learned the error of his ways, and worshipped a statue of his long-dead wife. Perdita, beautiful and marriageable, arrived at Leontes' court and was reunited with her repentant, foolish father. *Perdita*, I understood then, was the lost one found, the lucky child. I was pleased with my name, and did not think, those days, to read a wider allegory.

It was not until I was about eight, when Stella taught me the play in a home lesson, that I discovered that in Shakespeare's story Hermione is restored to life. Her statue unfreezes and she is miraculously alive. The stone rolled away. The blip-blip, blip-blip, on a lit screen somewhere, converting a lime flatline to a mountainous heartbeat. ("O, she's warm! If this be magic, let it be an art lawful as eating.") Hermione rediscovers the daughter she thought was ever-lost, and is instantly reconciled with her errant husband.

In her first telling my mother omitted this happy ending. I do not know if she really thought herself dead, or if my naming was truly circumstantial, the product of that desperate time in the downpour shack, when she thought herself dehumanised, negligible, a zero, when she lay listening to rain as if it was the sound of her own obliteration. The initial untruth of her telling was perhaps her truth; she was resigned to a life immobile and tyrannically fixed. She could have escaped my father but she did not, even when his contempt for her was ruthlessly evident. She stayed firmly put. I was an adult before I discovered there is no sea coast in Bohemia. Telling makes it so. All my childhood I believed in distant Bohemian beaches, where there might be wild bears, homicidally prowling.

*

When Nicholas returned from his week with Freddie Trevor, he discovered his little shack overtaken by women. For a few months he moved into the Trevors' house, and enjoyed there relative comfort and babyless quiet. And when Stella was moved to the hospital in Broome, it seemed all the more reasonable that he should stay where rational adults were, and not return to the bawling and the chatter and the black women, limp and sprawled on the floor of his shack, acting as if they owned it.

At the Trevors' Nicholas discovered that he could force the cook, Martha, and that she would not tell. All the white men did it; he felt manly and justified. At first he put his hand over her mouth, and watched her dark terrified eyes as he pushed hard into her. He made threats to kill her if she ever told. But gradually, he reasoned, Martha simply knew what to do; she believed his murderous threats and was sure to remain silent. Nicholas liked to pull her head back by its tangled hair and feel that he penetrated so that he hurt her. Martha was fifteen or sixteen years old and a wonderful cook, good as any, the Trevors claimed, in a civilised household. When, a few months later, Vera Trevor discovered that Martha was pregnant, she was sent away, down south, with few questions asked. The new cook, called Sheila, arrived almost immediately to replace her.

If there was any hesitation in Nicholas, moral or otherwise, it was one generated by the disquieting presence of Billy, the Trevors' youngest son. He was perhaps only eight or nine years old, but had about him the gravity of an older boy. He had the habit of appearing unexpectedly, as if spirited from place to place, and then he would just stand there, and stare, and unequivocally hum. If Billy was upset in any way he would often flap his hands, beating at his confusion, stirring up the air, attacking and shooing invisible entities. He had upstanding ginger hair and stippled greenish skin. Nicholas thought it best to ignore him, but sensed his persistent witness and censure; he felt a kind of violence towards Billy that he could imagine giving in to. He would throttle the boy if he could, seize him by the neck, fiercely crush the pink cord of his little-boy breath, and close everlastingly those insolent, staring, grey eyes. Only later did he learn that Billy was a deaf mute. If he had seen anything, well, he couldn't say. He was, Nicholas thought, more creature than boy, rightly contemptible.

When Stella returned from hospital, Nicholas moved back to the shack with his wife and their baby. They were an insecure family. Stella was quieter, still detached, but also given to barbed observation and general unhappiness. Her baby was a duty, her husband a fate to be suffered. Aboriginal women took Perdita into care for hours and Stella barely noticed her daughter's absence.

Nicholas decided he would make the best of things and become a famous anthropologist. He would crack open the code of primitive humanity, return to Cambridge triumphant, drink sherry with the dons, wear a long cardinal gown with an ermine trim, receive a silver badge on his chest, rosette-shaped, from the King, and an accolade detailing his discoveries, in full, in the *Sunday Times*.

He would write something incomparably difficult, fuelled with academic afflatus and magnificent prose. He wrote first to a bookshop in Sydney, ordering a crate of miscellaneous books, and began sketching out his own key to all mythologies, a work of dilatory, exalted oddity that he would never finish.

The books from Sydney, as it happened, saved Nicholas and Stella, and eventually their daughter would also discover them. Derangement of many forms finds its home within books. Stella was still self-consolingly reciting Shakespeare, especially the tragedies, and Nicholas, driven by the power of his compulsion to fame, was absent more often, away somewhere in his "field." But when they came together, appalled to be in each other's unmediated company, they could retreat, singly and sequestered, each into his or her own reading.

The books were stacked high against the walls, teetering in Babel piles. Nicholas never bothered to construct a bookshelf— he had not a handyman bone in his body—he simply leaned his books, as they accumulated, in random towers, never ordering or straightening, or even disposing according to subject. This is my memory of the furniture of our home. These books swelled in the moist heat and were prey to mice and to silverfish; an unlettering occurred, in titles, in spines. In some books only certain letters disappeared, as if an intelligent bug had taken offence at particular words; in others it was the edges of the pages that were consumed, so that they were lacy and partial, and left one to guess the lost sentence beginning every verso and the chewed sentence ending every recto. Snakes, attracted by the mice, liked to nest between the columns; we became accustomed to seeing an uncoiling as we dislodged a book from the back of the stacks. Stella was at first frightened, but became in the end so blasé about the supernumerous snakes that she kept a shovel nearby, so that she could flick them out the door as she was seeking her text. Sometimes, just out of annoyance, she cut them in two with the blade, disposing of them in a swift, elbow-jabbing, downward chop. It was a singular pleasure, she said, to see their writhing mad deaths.

By the time I was ten, when I began seriously to read—so that silent words, not utterance, would be my form of expression—half the front room was crowded by books. My narrow canvas stretcher was in the same room, against the side wall. I would fall asleep watching my parents read at the kitchen table, and if I woke in the night I found myself in this peculiar, librarian city, the massive architectonics of other people's words. Terraces, ziggurats, prominences and voids. In the darkness the pillars of books seemed to tilt and arch over me, yet I fancied not collapse, but a kind of shelter, the roof-shaped protection of open volumes.

After my father died, my mother became gradually more boldly explorative; she opened books that she had been forbidden to touch, sought out those marked specifically as his own. Because we were stranded together, and because I stuttered, we read. There is no refuge so private, no asylum more sane. There is no facility of voices captured elsewhere so entire and so marvellous. My tongue was lumpish and fixed, but in reading, silent reading, there was a release, a flight, a wheeling off into the blue spaces of exclamatory experience, diffuse and improbable, gloriously homeless. All that was solid melted into air, all that was air reshaped, and gained plausibility.

4

My early childhood was watched over by Sal and Daff, and by Billy Trevor. They called me Deeta. Sal and Daff continued, for several years, to work at the Trevors' house—a big station homestead, just a quarter of a mile up the track—but then Sal, and one month later Daff, disappeared with no warning. I was six, perhaps, when they abandoned me. I cried for days and days, as did Billy beside me, holding one of my hands while he flapped the other, like a broken bird-wing, like a trapped cockatoo, in a gesture of private and glum desolation.

By then they had taught me fragments of their language, Yawan, as well as a few basic words of my wet nurse's tongue. Before my stutter, I was a flexible and canny speaker, and I loved the full-mouthed sounds of indigenous nouns, the clever and precise onomatopoeia of the bird names, the cyclical songs, full of sonorous droning. And although I was a white-fella, a *kartiya*, Sal or Daff would carry me angled on their bony hips, and take me down to the creek-bed, to sit with their people.

I would be passed, like other small children, from body to body, nestling there, cradled in capacious laps, and I would feel the long fingers sift through my hair for lice, and the stroking of my arms, and the tickle of a tease. I was nourished and cared for in ways my parents were incapable of understanding. Sometimes Mrs. Trevor came striding down through the scrub to drag Billy and me away—mongrel no-hopers, she

called them, layabout blacks—but often we were simply forgotten and stayed where we were left.

From Sal and Daff I learned that my totem was a green tree
frog: many had appeared in the wet season, at the time of my
birth, and that this frog-fella, this one, this one was special to
me. "Im special-fella." Sal's totem was *puturu*, a grass seed that
her mother was gathering to grind for flour when she discovered she was pregnant. We didn't know what Daff's totem was;
she could not remember her mother. But there were spirits
everywhere that might enter a woman, and Mandjabari, the old
woman, said Daff one day might know.

"Spirits ebrywheres," she said. "Ebrywheres, all roun.'"

Billy, Billy was different; but the small group in the creek-
bed fed him and played with him and taught him skills with his
hands. The spirit within him was particular and probably
unknowable.

Only when I was older did I realise how much I loved Billy,
how faithful and consistent a companion he had been. He was
an odd-looking boy—pigeon-chested, with crooked teeth and
dappled skin. He had bottle-grey eyes, which he forgot to
blink, so that they often appeared watery, as if he was on the
verge of tears. These features made him look both stupid and
wise, and old-man Dauwarrngu said that Billy knew things,
secret things, like blackfellas, this one Billy-fella. Billy used to
like to plait my hair. The feel of his hands there, at my neck,
was like adoration. I have come to believe that we have lovers
all our lives, but only know them to be so if we remember the
specificities of touch.

*

In the smaller community of three, taut with conjugal unhappiness and the burden of an unacceptable child, Perdita witnessed other, more strained, human relations. In the scattered

light of afternoon she saw her parents argue—the smallest thing would make them ferocious with each other—and discovered that the ruins of a marriage are not necessarily quiet, but include yells, imprecations, megaphoned insults. The first time she saw Nicholas swing at Stella, striking her with an audible whack to the cheek, she ran outside, alarmed, to consider what had occurred. She fled into the bush and simply waited there until her own heart settled, crouching until there was such a quietness, an absorbing distinction and clarity to the look and feel of things, that she grew almost afraid. She was stirred by a rustle in the dry grass behind her and when she turned she saw three rust-coloured kangaroos, lazily grazing in the falling dusk. They were usually a glimpse, bounding away from the car, flinging themselves on their huge feet into bumpy flight, but now they were close, closer than ever before. Perdita liked the way their neat ears pivoted and twitched, catching her presence, and their upright arch, so casually alert. The large one scratched itself on the chest. Cocked its head. Eyed her sideways. And though she was sure it had seen her, it took its time leading the other two away, and then not in bounding, but in slow heavy hops, seesaw, rocking, raising small puffs of red dust from its padded heels.

Later Perdita felt ashamed that she had not rushed to her mother's side, and found that Stella was a stranger when she re-entered the house. Perdita heard her cursing in old-fashioned language; only afterwards would she know these were also the words of William Shakespeare, wrenched out of theatrical decorum to service a personal fury.

Nicholas sat at the table against the wall, smoking and reading and pretending his wife wasn't there. In the light of the kerosene lamp he looked weathered, tense. His profile had a sharp, *Sicilian* quality. *Leontes*. And the light glinting off his eyeglasses, Perdita thought, made him look sightless, brutal.

In bed that night, shadowed by the already growing city of

books, Perdita calmed herself by remembering the eyes of the large kangaroo: they were so lustrous and calm, so intrinsically lovely. Visitants, they were. Intercepting guests that might have had this message: the world is *also* still and calm and without collisions; the world is *also* these fond, benevolent presences, fur-warm and comforting, wanting nothing, silent.

*

Since her distrust of outsiders was more powerful than her hesitation of mothering, Stella would not allow her daughter to be sent away to school. So from the age of five, Perdita was taught at home, inefficiently, erratically, in fits and starts. When she was nine war was declared and Stella, in strange response, became orderly and purposeful. Nicholas left early each morning—as though he were a worker in a city bank, with a train to catch and a satchel of urgent papers to attend to—and then Stella, equally in need of a sustaining and fictitious timetable, waited exactly until 9 A.M. before the first lesson commenced. They would continue for three hours, then halt, even in mid-topic, on the dot of twelve, so that in the afternoons Stella could sleep, sew or read. She had drawn up a list of subjects—history, geography, religion, arithmetic, English, biology, Shakespeare, of course—which she reordered or dispensed with according to her inclination and mood, sometimes adding whatever book she had taken at random from their collection. That these books were adult and difficult seemed not to have occurred to her: and Perdita was both oppressed and delighted by what she could not understand, finding in every case at least a scrap of the comprehensible world. She wrote long lists of words she did not know the meaning of and promised herself that one day, in the future, she would know them all.

From her mother Perdita inherited an addled vision of the world; so much was unremembered or misremembered, so that the planet reshaped into new tectonic variations, changed the size and outline of countries on shaky hand-drawn maps, filled up with fabricated peoples and customs (many of them disquieting, weird, remote from understanding). History was English, and so was morality ("no elbows on the table" was a moral precept; "don't complain"; "don't lie"; "never tell strangers your real feelings"); so too, now that they were at war and the Hun were enemies again, the world had a protestant purpose and a democratic mission. Communism was evil, Perdita learned, more evil even than the Nazis, and the Godless Russians ate their own children during long frozen winters in which the sun, too defeated, simply slid along the horizon for a few hours before it returned everything to an icy, deathly darkness. Stella had coded the world into her own fierce antinomies, superpopulated with villains and evil-doers, fuelled by daft purpose and maniacal intention.

In the world of these lessons Stella and Perdita discovered, for the first time, an experience of intimacy. Perdita loved the imperative sound of her mother's voice, telling tales about everything under the sun. She loved her laugh, now and then, at her own descriptions, and the way she would embellish information with the slightest encouragement.

"How?" Perdita asked. "Why? Why not?"

Perdita watched her mother's mouth move, and heard what a wonder the mighty world was. Mother and daughter were united in what might be told and in the elastic possibilities of any telling.

The Shakespearean lessons were those Perdita loved best because they were stories. When her mother recited she was at a loss, completely bamboozled by the half-English, half-ornament quality of the verse, the overwrought pomposity of it all, the lavish sentiments. But when Stella first read aloud from Charles Lamb's summaries, the plots became intelligible, and Perdita was entranced by how terrible and how heroic people could be, by how many monarchs were mad, how many lovers disguised, how many women were faithless, or exceeding in beauty, how mistaken identity was everywhere and disastrously abroad, how easily stabbings or poisonings or suicides might occur, to shuffle off, Shakespeareanly, one's mortal coil. Stella had a particular affection for the tragedies, and a love of the soliloquies of Hamlet above all, so that by the time she was nine Perdita knew his most famous lamentations by heart:

> *O, that this too too solid flesh would melt,*
> *Thaw, and resolve itself into a dew!*
> *Or that the Everlasting had not fix'd*
> *His canon'gainst self-slaughter! O God! God!*
> *How weary, stale, flat and unprofitable,*
> *Seem to me the uses of this world!*
> *Fie on't! Ah, fie! 'tis an unweeded garden,*
> *That grows to seed, things rank and gross in nature*
> *Possess it merely. That it should come to this!*

Perdita was not entirely sure what this meant, but liked the animating grizzle, the bad-tempered tone. Stella declared that this speech, and others like it, were about "the big questions." She told her daughter that everything one needed to know about life was contained in a volume of Shakespeare; that he was all-wise, incomparable, the encompasser of every human range.

Even as a child Perdita knew this to be false. She stepped out into the dazzling light of Australia; she saw their blue kelpie, Horatio, scratching his balls in the angled cool shadow of the water tank; she saw zebra finches flash past, their black-white racing; she saw the Trevors' windmill at a distance, creakily turn, time-worn, straining, holding its iron wings cruciform; she felt hot wind brush her face and heard the hum of blowflies and the crackle of live things desiccating and the scamper of unseen lizards; all this life, all this huge unelaborated life, told her there was more on heaven and earth than was dreamt of by Mister Shakespeare.

There were dreaming spaces Mandjabari knew of, and old-man Dauwarrngu. There were even things her father knew of, with complicated names, and then there were all the unre-marked, simple and non-noble feelings, the taste of warm water dribbling from a canvas bag, the silky air of early evening shining with nickel-glow, the floaty feeling induced by hearing Aboriginal songs by firelight, and the rhythm of the clap sticks, repeating, and the words, the Language, drifting and braiding, drifting and braiding and dissolving into the darkness, like wind, like forgetting. *Small* questions, Perdita thought. There were *small* questions here. Or perhaps—the idea subversively filled her head—there were *different* big questions.

When she tried to discuss this with her mother, she was met by staunch refutation. Stella looked up from her sewing, a seer-sucker blouse with a row of tight crimson smocking, and said that some things in life were implicitly understood: the immor-tality of the soul, the mortality of the body and the peerless, exceptional, genius of Shakespeare. Beyond dispute, it was, wholly beyond dispute. She flapped the blouse fabric before her and examined it on her lap. Her fingers fiddled with a dan-gling thread, distinct as an artery. Beside her lay her sewing box, of wicker, and a biscuit tin of old buttons. Shakespeare had identified, she asserted again, *all* the "big" questions. Stella directed her hazel stare at her daughter and dared her to contradict. Perdita sensibly withdrew. She had, after all, known for a long time of her mother's idiosyncratic fixation and its suite of tough declarations on the meaning of life.

*

When he first arrived, Nicholas had spent a few hours each day with Willie, learning the tribal language of the region.

Since Willie was a stockman, paid in tobacco and flour, and certainly not paid more by Mr. Trevor to indulge this lazy-bugger whitefella, here for no reason and asking too many smart-aleck questions, Nicholas had to follow him at his work, and even to assist from time to time. As Willie roped steer and branded, made fence posts and erected them, chopped wood, carried water, fixed the bore and the windmill, dragged sacks of provisions and heaped them in the shed, as he broke horses, nailed nails, fashioned furniture from wood, Nicholas gradually collected a sparse vocabulary and a smattering of concepts; gradually too he began to admire the black man's hard labour, and his dignified care in the explanation of his own words. There were times Nicholas felt that Willie was holding back, not telling him everything, or even deliberately misinforming him on some crucial matter or other, but this was the characteristic treachery of the native he had been told to expect. In other terms, however, Willie was indispensable; Nicholas needed help for all that his book-learning had monumentally excluded.

By the time Perdita was about six, Nicholas had acquired enough knowledge to add to letters and reports to the Chief Protector of Aborigines the publication of the first of his meagre output of academic articles. He privately realised now that he would never become a famous intellectual, such as he had seen pointed out, crossing the lawns at Cambridge, moving in long gowns with magisterial self-importance, burnished by citational prestige and university gossip. Nor would his contribution to Aboriginal ethnography be anything other than a crude transliteration of stories, and the more useful, perhaps more respectable, delineation of language systems and kin groups, much of which, in the end, he garnered from Mr. Trevor. Like his wife, Nicholas had developed a passivity in relation to his own life. He lost track of time; he lost purpose and ambition; the barest professional pretext enabled him to stay in a country in which he had unconscionably, disastrously, lost himself. He saw that *Perdita*, the lost one, was the member of his family who most seemed unlost.

Now and then Nicholas received letters from his ageing father—asking him, begging him, to return home with his family, offering inducements, the managership, once again, of the largest store—but these consolidated his sense of estrangement and disaffection. He despised his father for having given him so much, for his unending solicitude and irritating hopefulness. "My son," the letters always began. He had, moreover, no compunction in asking his father for money (which always arrived, monthly, with more filial begging), but felt that while he remained abroad he was free from the haberdashery destiny Mr. Keene senior would foist on him. To his father he sent letters composed entirely of fictions, suggesting he was on the edge of a scholarly breakthrough, that his work would have a universally relevant importance, discovering, as it must, the base infancy of man. His paper would become known as "The Keene Hypothesis."

When war was declared in 1939, Nicholas was excited until he discovered he had been denied a commission; his fiction then was that he worked in British Army Intelligence, engaged on some kind of clandestine mission. But he would return to England, he decided, as soon as the war was over.

Locals in Broome thought Nicholas Keene a fraud and a bloody no-hoper; no one seemed to know what the hell he was doin'. Wastin' time, prob'ly. Muckin' round. Voices laconically gossiped on pub verandas: why that pommy bloke hung about, anyhows, in that buggered little shack, with his mad-crazy missus and his gone-feral kiddie, was anyone's guess.

5

Something happened, something broke, in Perdita's eleventh year, in 1940. Stella, normally garrulous, stopped talking al-together, and fell again into her own deep cavernous emptiness, all compulsive interrogation but with no answers to "big questions." She yawned all the time, and would not make eye contact. She stopped washing and eating, she picked un-detectable specks from her dirty clothes. She said there was a huge, deafening uproar sounding in her ears, like crowds jostling for their carriage in St. Pancras Station, and the clang of metal there, and the resounding platform, and heavy iron machinery slowing down or speeding up, and the hissing emissions of steam from corroded lead pipes. People were shouting, she said, and whistles were blowing. Too many people were shouting. Nicholas also shouted at Stella, but it seemed to make no difference. He found her recalcitrant unhappiness an affront, a disgrace.

Perdita could not really imagine "St. Pancras Station." It may have been like the inside of the engine of Mr. Trevor's truck, only much, much bigger. Some kind of rattling contraption, hot and agitated. In England, she knew, there existed colossal chambers of stone and metal, buildings in which a hundred people might stand together at one time. In such a place it made sense that everyone would be shouting; there would be crowded anxieties, dropped parcels and small lost children; there would be tormenting intrusions and no easy exits. Whatever her mother experienced must be truly dreadful. Perdita looked at her turning a teacup, again and again, by its comma-shaped handle. She felt a sudden wave of love and concern, a feeling rare enough, but for which she was grateful. What linked them persisted in the emotional residues of what had been taught, the tales they mentally engaged with, the flights of fancy.

Nicholas decided that Stella needed more time away, in the hospital, in Broome. She had "lost something," he said, and Perdita wondered what *thing* it was. Certainly, Stella was possessed of an unnerving silence. Words, thought Perdita. Perhaps it was words she had lost. When they packed to leave, all Stella wanted with her was her biscuit tin of loose buttons. She clasped it to her chest as if it were a book, or a baby.

Although by then Nicholas had his own Jeep, the trip into town was in Mr. Trevor's half-worn-out truck. Nicholas and Stella sat with Mr. Trevor in the tight little cabin, and Perdita sat with their luggage in the tray, in the dust and sun, jolted at every turn. Through a rectangle of grimy glass she could see the backs of their heads, bobbing like dolls, like strangers, as if inorganic and unattached, and she wondered how long her mother's absence might be, and if, after this illness, she would recover at all. Mrs. Trevor, leaning her flushed face forward, talking in serious adult tones, had told Perdita that her mother just needed another rest; just for a little while, she said, where nurses could look after her. But Perdita knew there was hideous desolation there somewhere. This was not simple tiredness but some bigger, unmentionable fatigue-with-life, something that opened the mind up to a railway station and invading crowds.

The visions on that journey were those that will return all her life. It is not that anything Perdita saw was unfamiliar; it is that they were trailed out, spool-like and consecutive, for future memory, that they were marked by the poignancy and rarity of the occasion—taking her mother away, for who knew how long—and the sense, some intuited, anxious and desperate sense, of the injustice of her disposal, and of its necessity.

From the tray of the old truck, bruised with the wallop of too rough a journey, Perdita watched the shuddering world pass by—boab trees here and there, their bellies distended, their stick limbs dead stiff, scratching at the sky, the sculptural forms of anthills, also quasi-human, flashes of morning light broken by scraggly trees and granite outcrops, random uprisings of startled birds, fleeting shapes that might have been wallaby, a lone bullock, far away, hurtling crazily through the open scrub; all this travelling landscape, all this mobile world, seemed somehow impressed with the solemnity and purpose of their journey. Behind them, a cloud of orange dust mushroomed and spun with the turbulence Perdita understood as catastrophe.

In town Nicholas and Perdita stayed at the Continental Hotel. Perdita loved the long verandas and the wide-open shutters and the inside beer garden, shaded by multicoloured umbrellas. A small Malay man in a sarong and headscarf led them to their adjacent rooms. He bobbed and bowed as he opened the doors. They had beds with clean linen; they had running water and electric lights. Perdita slumped onto her bed, feeling as if she had been battered. There were bruises on her buttocks and knees from the journey, and she felt a sting in the corner of her eye that she knew was the beginning of an infection. Instructed to stay in her room while her mother was taken to the hospital, Perdita simply lay, relieved to have the world at last stop still, worried that she had not said goodbye to her mother. She dozed a little, on the cool soap-smelling sheets: *Lifebuoy*. A breeze infused by ocean salt threaded through the shutters.

When Perdita awoke she was hungry and went exploring. In a small wooden shed out the back she located a kitchen, and a kind woman bent towards her, touched her cheek ceremoniously, and offered her a breakfast of toast and fried eggs.

The woman—Sis, her name was—ministered sustenance

and gentleness to whomever wandered lost into her modest kitchen. Sis was from Beagle Bay Mission and had family all over, she said, all over the place, ebrywheres, ebrywheres roun here. She had married a Japanese pearl diver; they had six children, she announced proudly, now all grown up strong. Perdita replied, sounding earnest, that she was an only child, but that there was Billy, her friend, who was maybe like a brother, even if he was a Trevor, and simple, and could not hear or speak at all. She watched the woman's body move sideways, drying dishes, stacking them.

Then Sis turned to her and said suddenly, "Your dad, I seen him roun. But your mum. Is she still alive?"

Perdita was shocked that this stranger might have imagined her mother dead. Or might know something.

"Hospital," she said blankly. "Mum's sick. In the head."

This did not describe the noisy railway station, or the competing silence, or the mysterious depleting languor to which her mother was now subject. But Sis looked calmly at her and nodded.

"Ah, yeah," she said, her tone sympathetic, as if she knew, in any case, what a railway station might feel like, and what might visit an unfortunate woman like a fist-blow in the dark. Perdita held up her dirty plate, smeared with egg yolk and frilly scraps. Sis took it with both hands and plunged it in brown soapy water.

"Thanks, missus," Perdita said, genuinely grateful.

"No worries."

Sis turned back to her and sweetly smiled.

When Nicholas returned from the hospital he seemed cheerier somehow. He moved like a man without shrapnel lodged in his back, a man young, unencumbered. In the bar of the Continental Hotel he made weak attempts at jokes, and the locals, knowing already about the mad wife and the reason for his town visit, humoured and indulged him. Perdita sat perched unsteadily on a bar stool, sipping a glass of lemonade. She had rarely seen her father in new company; he seemed inept, but trying hard. As it grew darker she watched him become inebriated; she watched how he leaned on the bar, resting his body there, how his features sagged and transformed, how he gulped as if greedy. At one stage he knocked over a glass of whisky and immediately ordered another, downing it super-swift. He had forgotten she was there. Perdita counted the bottles above the bar, listened to the laughter of drunk men, saw her own reflection, squeamish, in a long wavy mirror etched on the surface with toppling palms. Such a pale small face, such a tentative oval.

Some time later a buxom barmaid, a beautiful woman with slanted eyes and a marcelled hairdo, took Perdita by the hand and led her along the passageway to her room. She left her with a smacking kiss and a packet of salted peanuts.

"Sleep, luv," she instructed, as she closed the door behind her.

Perdita thought she would visit Sis, but decided she was too tired, much too tired. Her sore eye was gumming over and had begun slowly to throb. She lay in her clothes and sandals on her luxurious bed, very still, very alone, thinking for some reason, though it was sultry and dank, of her mother's dream of snow. One day, she decided, she would see snow for herself. She would go to England, or Russia, far, far away. Russia. Yes, Russia. She would go to distant Russia and see the snow. But in the meantime, her mother's dream had become her own private treasure; she fell asleep imagining a soft drift, an endless vertical sadness, a delicate slow sinking, a whiteness, a whiteness.

*

Nicholas and Perdita were both woken by the call of butcher birds in a nearby tamarind tree, and by a clanking metallic sound that turned out to be a group of Aboriginal men in iron chains, linked painfully by their ankles. They had been released from gaol to make bitumen roads. From the small window of her hotel room Perdita saw them, men joined in this way, humiliated, caught, and wondered what they had done to be so cruelly constrained. They wore ragged trousers and grimy singlets; their faces shone in the sunshine. A prison guard was sitting at a distance under the blue shade of the mango tree, pinching a cigarette into shape, licking it, turning it, slowly striking a match. He inhaled deeply, watching all the while. When Perdita and her father left the hotel, she realised that she recognised one of the chained men. It was Kurnti, who sometimes worked in the stockyard at the Trevors' station. Perdita called his name and waved, and he straightaway waved back, his face offering up a truly innocent smile.

"Deeta!" he called out. "Yah, Deeta!"

Nicholas turned to look, but did not say anything. He simply seized his daughter's wrist and dragged her away.

Perdita carried through the day the image of a black man waving. The smell of hot tar. The clunk of heavy chains. The sound of her own name called out to her, as if it was Aboriginal.

*

That day Nicholas took her to a convent. It was a large wooden building, lined with shutters. Black and white faces in wimples peered at them curiously as they walked together up the gravel driveway, lined with purple bougainvillaea. In the front room, where they were told to wait in silence, there was a large crucifix on the wall, which Perdita stared at, fascinated. Christ had a face of famished hollows and softly closed eyes, and a look of calm, self-satisfied repose. Perdita remembered Stella's stories, explicit and unbelievable. She wondered suddenly if Nicholas planned to leave her here, with these stiff, wimpled women in triangular dresses who worshipped this wretched, assassinated king. She experienced a moment of panic; why was she never told anything? Why did adults, always and anyhow, get to make all the decisions?

Perdita was about to ask when a nun called Sister Immaculata led a young woman into the room: Mary. She had bronze-coloured skin and deep black eyes. She stood a little apart, as if in a different world from the convent sisters. Mary was sixteen years old, tall for her age, and had about her an air of maturity and self-possession. Perdita shyly smiled. The smile was more confidently returned. Nicholas explained that Mary had been raised in a Catholic orphanage down south, and that she would be coming to live with them, to cook and to clean, and to help with lessons, while her mother was away. Mary could read, he added. Sister Immaculata performed a little bow and Perdita wondered if her father was someone important. Then the sister lurched forward, all of a sudden, and took Perdita's face in her hands.

"Dear, oh dear," she said, staring into her infected eye.

She ordered the child to stay put as she fetched some ointment. Perdita felt the long explorative fingers of the nun, arthritic and witchy, holding open her eye as she applied translucent cream from a tiny metal tube. The nun's thumbs rested beneath her right eye, then her left. Perdita was afraid. She understood the healing intention, but still she felt afraid. Both eyes were streaming uncontrollably with tears. At some point in the procedure Mary took her hand and stayed close, instantly affectionate, in an implicit companionship. It was a fond, easy handclasp. Perdita felt the lacing of their fingers. This was the moment, the very moment, that Perdita began to love Mary.

*

On the return journey Nicholas and Mr. Trevor sat in the

cabin, and Mary and Perdita sat in the tray of the truck, sharing their space with boxes and crates of stores the men had
bought. Before they left town they had been on a shopping
trip to Streeter and Male, the general store, and had bought
canned milk, cereals, biscuits, corn. At Fongs they had bought
a sack of rice, and Perdita had wanted to linger there, where
the exotic resided. Then at the bakery they had purchased a
few loaves of still-warm bread. This was an unusual treat for
Perdita; her mother never baked bread and she had rarely
tasted it fresh.

The truck broke down ten miles short of its destination. Mr.
Trevor and Nicholas stood with their heads under the bonnet,
fiddling with the fan belt. They tapped on the radiator with a
spanner, and talked in technical whispers. Adjustments were
made, the engine attended to. It click, click, clicked, as by
degrees it slowly cooled. Mary and Perdita sat in the dirt eating bread and honey, tipped directly from a brand-new jar,
spread with their fingers. Flies swarmed all around, buzzing,
insistent, but they simply ignored them and ate like they were
starving. Perdita would have stuffed herself if she could. She
would have taken it all in, every substance and sweetness. She
would have filled herself so that there were no spaces left that
her mother-memory could inhabit. At some point Mary leaned
towards Perdita and with her little finger wiped a trail of honey
from the side of her mouth, then licked her own finger clean,
winked and smiled.

"Sisters, eh?" Mary said.

Perdita felt—what was it?—claimed, rescued. She smiled
with her own mouth full of sticky bread and felt her small,
unnoticed life reconfiguring around her.

By the time the vehicle was back on the road, its old engine
cranked by an iron handle into a cantankerous rumble, darkness was falling. Birds were roosting in the twilight, restless,
then settling; Perdita could see their bleary shapes on the

bloodwoods and high in the gums. A flock of galahs rose flapping, then noisily descended. Mr. Trevor kindly drove his passengers right to their door. In the bluish evening Perdita saw the outline of their shack loom up, then heard Horatio hurl towards them, frantic with welcoming joy. He rushed at her so energetically, his dog-life effusive and exploding, that he knocked her flat.

*

What return was it, that night, with no mother, with Mary?

I have thought of it, over the years, not as a substitution—since one person can never, after all, replace another—but as the portentous sign of things made dangerously misaligned. Mary was not a mother, but a sister; there was still Stella's absence, and my inexpressible, almost inadmissible, missing her. I wondered every day about where exactly she was, what treatment she was receiving. I imagined a handsome doctor in a white gown, giving her an injection in the upper arm as she gazed, distracted, into the middle distance. Her hair was brushed back in even furrows; she wore a simple nightgown of faded pink. It was a generic, dull image, from who-knows-where, but somehow I found it reassuring.

Despite the fact that I was unconvinced of her love (since she had never been a mother who might embrace, or kiss, or reach inadvertently to caress), there was the stringent complicity of our isolation and the far-fetched world of notions we had daily shared. Perhaps I attached to her snow dream so passionately because it was something personal, some token of a truly inner life she would rarely reveal.

My father groped in the darkness as Mary and I stood at the door. Horatio was still jumping up, not yet ready to be calm, his fast panting exaggerated in the still of the night. Mary reached again for my hand, as if this time it was she who needed the comfort of touch. We heard something fall with a heavy thud—knocked-over books, no doubt—then a scratching and a fumbling. At length the bloom of a kerosene lamp uprose in the darkness, and with it came my father's face, swelling into view, burnished and brass-coloured above the flame he was controlling with his thumb and index finger. The lenses of his spectacles once again took away his eyes, leaving behind twin discs of light. I saw him there, half present, blurred in groggy distance, as if at the end of a tunnel. I pushed Horatio down, gave him a quick smack on the nose to quiet him, and then led Mary, trembling, into our illuminated home.

It looked so small, now, after the room in the Continental Hotel, almost suffocating, and with a heavy odour of dust. A spray of cockroaches fanned open and scuttled into corners. But there was book-scent, and things known, and our shadows in the lamplight, the dog waiting to be fed, the unpacking of the day's purchases. Mary was passive, doing exactly what she was told. I remember that my father gave her a place to sleep beside me, on the floor. He unrolled a canvas swag, and without a word took the kerosene lamp with him and went into the bedroom. The pool of light that he dragged behind him was closed off, contained, becoming a thin bright seam pressed beneath the bedroom door.

Mary was silent; she lay herself down. Even then I felt that something was wrong. Outside a wind started up, a slack moaning wind.

PART TWO

DOCTOR: Foul whisperings are abroad. Unnatural deeds
Do breed unnatural troubles; infected minds
To their deaf pillows will discharge their secrets . . .

Macbeth, V i

6

In the world beyond, 1940 was aflame with nations in crisis. The Nazis had invaded the Netherlands, Belgium and Luxembourg; the blitzkrieg had caused the British retreat at Dunkirk; Luftwaffe and Messerschmitt were dive-bombing the Homeland. Perdita heard all this, all this new military language, riveted with metallic names and foreign locations, from her increasingly remote and war-obsessed father. Although he received newspapers two weeks late from Perth, and then only when Mr. Trevor made a trip to town, Nicholas was following the war with an almost scholarly attention. Manoeuvres, tactics, victories, defeats: these excited and frustrated him, made him feel both involved and dreadfully excluded.

He found himself dreaming again of 1918, and yearning for the thunder of tanks advancing and the sheer terror that made grown men, men like himself, shit and puke and call out to God or their mothers in excited extremity. In a repeated dream he leaped over trenches with the stride of a long-jumper, seeing beneath him strewn bodies and grisly death. He carried his rifle, bayonet fixed, up high above his shoulders, keeping it poised horizontally as he had been taught to do, but he never seemed to land on the other side of the trench. He was stuck there, like a corpse in a ridiculous pose. Stuck there in thunderous dreamland, in exploding mid-air.

Perdita remembers the day, in July, when her father announced that the Germans one month ago had entered Paris. His eyes glittered maniacally; she almost felt afraid of him. How could the distant war invade in this way? Nicholas told his daughter that it was only a matter of time before Australia would be attacked, and that he would be summoned, in a leadership role, to defend the hapless Australians from the evil Hun and their allies. There would be unimaginable suffering, he said, and hideous mutilations. There would be air raids and bombings. The sky itself would burn. As he sipped his tea, gleefully misanthropic, Perdita and Mary exchanged frightened glances. He was like a shadow they lived under. He had become darkened and impersonal.

*

It would remain wholly separate, Perdita's time with Mary. There was something implacable, sure, about what they shared. Mary was by turns girlish and adult, but she looked after Perdita, daily attending her, offering companionship, knowledge and canny advice. She taught her poker (how to shuffle, to deal, how, finally, to cheat), desert songs (learned from her mother from whom she'd been taken), and the lives of the saints (the strange details of which she had read about in the orphanage). She taught Perdita, and Billy too, how to locate *pitjuri*, bush tobacco, and to chew it until the sides of their cheeks began to tingle and salivate, so that they experienced its sour, stimulating effects. She showed them the chevron sand-lines of lizards, identifying the species, and taught them how to track back, hunting stealthily, to a log hole or a burrow. The ripples of departed snakes, the scroll shapes and mounds and pathways of bush tucker—all that had been inscribed there before them, in a hidden language never noticed, became suddenly visible.

"Whitefellas can't see nothin' around them; whitefellas all buggered up in the head," Mary declared, touching her temple. "'Cept you two, of course," she added with a broad grin.

Under her intelligent guidance the scrub, which had seemed so empty, took on fullness and detail. Every bird had a true name, every mark in the wind-scalloped dirt betokened liveliness and activity. Even the glass-clear sky was a fabric of signs. There were seasons that a whitefella never noticed, marked by tiny efflorescences and the swelling and fading of bush fruit. Mary also knew about the stock on the station— which of the cattle were calving, which horses were slow or ill-tempered, which she wanted the opportunity to ride.

Billy and Perdita were both charmed by Mary. She was cleverer—and funnier—than anyone they had ever met.

They were hanging out washing together, each under a scratchy straw hat, when Perdita asked Mary to tell her story. Billy was nearby, lying in the dirt with Horatio, tickling the dog's belly as he parted his quivering legs. It helped her speak, perhaps, the fact that Billy was deaf, that he smiled up at her as she spoke, with little knowledge of her words. Mary was Walmajarri, she said, from near Fitzroy Crossing. Her people were desert people. Her mother was Dootharra and her father was a white stockman, a *kartiya*, no name, buggered off, somewheres, long time, nobody knows, somewheres, longaway. Her people had gone to a feeding station to get flour and tobacco, then someone from the Government, seeing her pale skin, seized her from her mother and took her to Balgo Mission. She cried and cried. She said that her mother spoke to her in the wind, and that she was crying too, full of whispery breath, overflowing and spreading out, coming like wind-spirit across the land to find and to claim her. But it was no good, they never saw each other again. Mary was six years old when she was taken away. Mission fellas noticed that she was unusually smart, so later, two years later, she was sent down south, to an orphanage in the city called Sister Clare's. To learn to be a whitefella, she said, to learn all them whitefella ways.

"Thank you, Sister, yes, Sister. A cup of tea, Sister. Please, Sister."

There was a comic mischief, a shrewd pleasure, to Mary's skilled mimicry. She shifted accents and registers; her tales held echoes and ironies. Perdita had never heard anyone speak so openly before, or, for that matter, in so many different voices. When Mary recently returned to the north, to the convent in Broome, she heard from blackfellas passing through that her mother had died. Dootharra had rolled into a campfire one night and was too tired, or too sad, maybe, to roll out again. Her skin was burned, she was lost, she was a dark, dark shade. Mary found a rock and struck at her head until it bled, to show in the Walmajarri way her grieving for her mother, to feel it truly and painfully. The nuns had seen her, and scolded her. They said her behaviour was unChristian. She had looked down at the blood-drops on the earth and wanted her own death.

"I wanted," said Mary, "to send my voice into the wind, to fly to her, to go away, to go long, longaway."

Mary slumped to the ground, as if unbuckled, and began to cry. There, beneath the flapping shirts and dresses, the thin cotton garments made warm and lit by the sunshine, lemon-coloured, slight and wispy as ghosts, she fell down and wept. Billy was shocked by this sadness, come so suddenly, that he did not understand. He began to flap his hands, swatting at the air, then to moan, and then in sympathy also to weep. Horatio turned on to his belly, paws outstretched, and looked imploringly unhappy, as dogs sometimes do. And though she was the youngest and smallest, Perdita reached her arms around Mary and Billy and gathered them in; and their little group, like another family, inclined lovingly together, couched in the comfort of hot bodies in a clumsy child's embrace.

*

At night, after Nicholas took the kerosene lamp into the bedroom, to read in peace, or to study the war, or to write his colossal "Keene Hypothesis," Mary and Perdita often lay close together and talked in the darkness. Mary was intrigued by the city of stacked books—which she would eventually start to read herself—but remarked that the library did not seem to include a Bible, nor her favourite, most scary book.

"Good stories. Proper stories," Mary said with emphasis.

When she had first arrived in the city she was given a bundle of belongings: two gingham dresses, two pairs of underpants, one woollen sweater and green leather sandals. In a brown paper bag there was, in addition, a pair of wire-rimmed spectacles, a gold cross on a chain, and a thick blue-covered book, *The Lives of the Saints*. Inside the cover was a name, "Annie McCaughie." She had died, Sister Benedict said, of measles or diphtheria; she was With Our Lord, Resting in Peace, and her parents had generously donated her possessions to the Aboriginal orphanage.

From Annie McCaughie's book, Mary learned about the ghastly profession of sainthood. Saints were devoted to God, with extravagant piety, but then equally fated, most of them, to die deaths of hyperbolic and nonsensical suffering. The women, in particular, were predestined in this way, their holiness determined, it seemed, by the measure of their earthly torments. Mary told Perdita the outlines of the stories. St. Agatha, having refused the attentions of a Roman prefect in Sicily, was tortured by being hung upside down and having her breasts twisted from her body. She is represented holding her severed breasts before her, lumpish and bloody, on a golden tray, evidence of her virginal courage. St. Apollonia, deaconess of Alexandria, who defended her faith against marauding anti-Christians, had all her teeth knocked out in a brutal attack and was pictured displaying her dislodged, dental motifs resting in her lap. (She was, Mary added, the patron saint of dentists and the saint to whom one prays in times of toothache.) St. Lucy, who suffered the gouging out of her eyes, was depicted holding them on a plate, or in a purse, or dangling gruesomely from a stalk like two ripe cherries.

Perdita listened in horror to the stories Mary retold. She had never imagined—even in the theatrical surplus of a Shakespearean tragedy, glutted with sensation—that women could be treated in this way, torn apart and made holy by tremendous injustice and error.

"I know more saints," Mary had whispered, her voice deep and warm under the cover of darkness, and Perdita was both curious and afraid to learn more of what humans might do to each other. Annie McCaughie's book, Mary said, had also been hers: it had a page of tissue paper at the front, covering a depiction of St. Stephen, the protomartyr, being stoned to death, and a cover embossed in the centre with a circle of gold doves. Inside there were many coloured illustrations, all on the same thick glossy paper, all behind a thin layer of tissue paper, which made each viewing seem a singular disclosure. Perhaps for Mary there was some solace in thinking that suffering might have a spiritual purpose. Or perhaps nothing, in the end, matched the atrocity of a distant mother rolled into a fire, so lost in grief, and so irremediably heartbroken, that she did not care to remove her burning self from the unholy flames.

*

There were forms of knowledge of the land and the body, carried into adulthood, that Perdita learned especially, and only, from her sister, Mary. Often they would simply walk— Mary said sitting inside for too long was like a kind of sleep— and in their wandering, sometimes with Billy Trevor trailing behind, humming to himself in his own quiet world, sometimes with Horatio trotting and sniffing this way and that way ahead, they traded stories and stored up secrets. The twitchy and particular life of animals was of interest to Mary, and she was always aware of the barest movement, of dry grass bending, a rustly stir, the traces and suggestions of other live presences. Her totem was the honey ant: she knew where they nested. With her digging stick she would extract them, and present Billy and Perdita with squirming black-and-amber handfuls. They would suck the backs off the honey ants—popping their sweet abdomens in the cavities of their mouths—while she watched them, pleased. Mary never ate the honey ant herself; it was her creature, hers.

In the western desert, said Mary, there were still some blackfellas who had never yet seen the *kartiya*, people, her people, dressed only in hair-strings and feathers and treading lightly across the earth. They carried water bags of red wallaby skin, spears and digging sticks. They knew everything, she said, everything about the world, every big important thing, and every single little thing.

Perdita thought a great deal about these people, wondering what they knew. The *big* questions. The *other* questions. She had seen a desert man in Broome once, sitting propped against a tree, looking lost and alone. He had scars in raised lines cut into his chest and wore a bright ornament of pearl shell around his neck, threaded on hair. Nicholas had pointed him out and said he was an important man of Law. He *knew things*, her father said, that he would describe and uncover.

Sometimes Mary, Billy and Perdita would sit in a triangle, facing each other, for no reason at all but to feel the wind on their faces and wait, utterly still, until bird-life visited them. There were flaring budgerigars and sulphur-crested cockatoo; sometimes there was a hawk, lazily circling, or a fleet cloud of bush pigeon, heading towards the sun. Perdita learned to ignore the flies clustering in the corners of her eyes, or on the picked ugly scabs of her elbows and knees. She learned from

Mary that if you lick stones they colourfully shine—agate, chrysoprase, rose-coloured quartz—that if you put your ear to the dirt you can hear footsteps miles away, and buried life going on, somewhere underground, that there are waterholes, *jila*, hidden in the desert country that the *kartiya*, the whitefella, will never see. There was an entire universe, she was discovering, of the visible and the invisible, the unconcealed and the concealed, some fundamental hinge to all this hotchpotch, disorderly life, this swooning confusion. For Mary there was authority in signs Perdita had never before seen; there were pronouncements in tiny sounds and revelations in glimpses. Vast, imperishable life was everywhere apparent; accretion, abrasion, the unthwarted growing of small things. The stars were there all the time, Mary said, outstretching her arms; we just couldn't see them all the time. This seemed to Perdita an amazing notion. She thought of stars adjusting, each night, their luminous arrangements, then effacing, disappearing, hiding behind day. Why had she never known things like this before? She wondered what God was, and whether he was there, or necessary.

*

One night Perdita woke from deep sleeping to hear strange sounds. The door of her father's room was ajar, so that a wedge of thin sallow light streamed in towards her bed. Perdita rose and half-asleep walked to peer through her father's doorway. Nicholas was hurting Mary. She saw the humped form of her father's back and heard him grunting and pounding, and she could hear from the shadow beneath him the sound of Mary softly weeping. Perdita was not really sure what it was that she saw, what night vision had visited, bent into shapes and sounds, a dream perhaps, uncertain, askew, incomprehensible. She retreated to her bed. She did not want to know. She turned her face to the wall and shut her eyes tight.

What witness was this, that Perdita could not bear to contemplate? What palpitation of the heart, what sense of panicked strangulation, was she suppressing behind her tightly closed eyes? Perdita was frightened. The night was dark. With her eyes closed there was an extra darkness she could sink her witnessing into.

7

Just as Stella had the railway station booming within her, Nicholas, Perdita thought, might be said to have a war inside him. After the Battle of Britain he talked more frequently of the war, but it was the Blitz, in particular, that most aroused his excitement. In the air offensive on 15 September, Southampton, Manchester, Bristol, Liverpool and Cardiff were all bombed. Nicholas talked of Hawker Hurricanes and Supermarine Spitfires. He spoke of thin-fingered searchlights clutching at the sky, of anti-aircraft fire sparking in all directions, of explosions, smoke, civilians burned to cinders in their demolished homes. Calamity was glorious, tragedy was seductive. Something in the shattering of substance attracted and inspired him. Perdita knew he wanted to be in London to see it falling down about him, to sniff death and to enjoy the disaster of warfare. Cuttings from the *Western Mail* began appearing tacked to the walls: grainy and imprecise vistas, buildings aflame beneath flourishes of smoke, figures huddled in bomb shelters, sometimes with insect-like masks, a German plane—one of the most imprinting and memorable images of all—heading downwards, like a crucifix, straight into the earth.

In this remote part of the planet that was Perdita's centre, where there was no electricity, or school, or modern-day conveniences, the war visited in these textual and solemn ways. Here, where there were three dimensions and irrevocably solid things, where bodies sweated and were scratched and smeared by the world, where there were fires at night, and insects, and banal forms of loneliness, and noise no louder than that of thunder and of rain on a galvanised roof, the newspaper cuttings were like movie stills, fake-looking and stagy.

One day Billy put his face in the doorway and his eyes grew large. Perdita saw at once how very unusual their little dwelling had become, all books, all symbolic strife, the missing mother, the remote father.

Billy would not enter the room but simply stood there, staring, his eyes scanning the Blitz photographs as they trembled in a slight breeze, his expression baffled. His large hands began slowly to bat the air. In the accustoming texture of childhood, where the startling becomes the expected, and parental peculiarity is adapted to the everyday, Perdita had few experiences of imagining her home from the outside. Billy, who spoke no words, but simply looked with exceptional gravity, and told his responses through the wayward movements of his body, gave her pause. It was the first understanding, perhaps, that her parents were locked in their obsessive devotions, that only Mary, finally, could be relied upon to notice her, her own small life, there in the background, her own small, unfinished life, with all its huge, aching questions.

*

Although Mary had told Nicholas that she was conducting regular lessons, in truth she was not. Lessons, such as they were, were random and occasional. Perdita knew many things Mary had never heard of and Mary had other resources Nicholas would never have guessed. Perdita enjoyed telling Mary the story of her name: it sounded astonishing as she told it. A mad Sicilian, a wronged mother, an enchanted woman-statue, paranormally—magically!—brought back to life; the child with her name abandoned on the bear-infested sea coast of Bohemia.

"Antigonus is eaten," said Perdita, "but the baby girl is saved."

"Saved," Mary repeated.

"Yes, saved. She returns to her father. She makes her mother live."

Mary looked interested.

"Like magic," insisted Perdita.

As she told the tale Perdita realised that what she liked most was its ending; so that although there was a rage of passion, a convulsion of injustice, a good man eaten offstage by a savage bear, there was also restoration, stability, a royal family reunited.

Mary also liked the story, particularly the part about the statue coming to life. In the chapel at the orphanage in Perth, she said, there was a statue of the Madonna that sometimes shivered and wept. One of the nuns had seen it. The Madonna wore a long blue robe covered with gold painted stars and had affixed to its plaster head an elliptical halo of lights. These were switched on for important occasions. Mary had watched and watched, waiting after prayers, silent and respectful, her head bowed in penitence as specially instructed, but had never seen—not a bit—any shivering or weeping.

In blackfella stories, Mary said, things changed all the time: a tree into a woman, a woman into a tree. There were rocks that had been children and stars that talked. Spirit was everywhere, she insisted, not just in a church.

Perdita, who felt spiritless, wished she believed something. Behind her thinking there existed a perishing twilight, a sense of outer space, of nothing really there. She thought of this nothing as a kind of hazy, wreathing smoke, floating upwards, away. A nothing like starless night. A nothing eyes-closed took you into.

Later Perdita would learn with fretful misery how useless was her knowledge. Her mother's history and geography were wild surmise, her politics were eccentric to the point of crude error; even her Shakespeare was a nonsense, partial accomplishment, a clutter of stories and quotations, an ingenious but lamentably archaic vocabulary, the integument of exile, neurosis, migrant sadness. This maternal inheritance, more than anything, would serve to humiliate her.

But Mary's gentle teaching—all that drifted to her in the darkness when they were lying close together, all that was told on a walkabout, with Billy and Horatio accompanying, benignly, happily, both of them running ahead, all the unfortunate saints, and the bush knowledge, and the shared stories of mothers—these things remained securely lodged, and vouched safe.

This small remembered moment: Mary had Billy and Perdita sit on the front step, a pile of gathered seed pods nestling between them. The pods were long and curved, like a Turkish man's slipper, and crisp as if baked like potatoes in the oven. In each seed pod were rows of tiny black and red seeds, so shiny you might have believed they were painted with acrylics. *Jequirity seeds.* Together they strung the seeds on lengths of cotton thread, each fashioning a necklace. As they worked, Mary sang a song in her own language, a few words of which—"wind," "mother," "fire"—Perdita caught as they drifted past, fragile and dispersing as ash. Lamentation was like this, a falling thing, something in the air itself, something flighty and incalculable. When the necklaces were made the three wore them as a sign of their bond, their own little tribe. This moment of making will remain after everything else collapses: fingers, voice, the summoning unity of three souls.

*

Mrs. Trevor looked in on them from time to time. Her son Billy was spending less time at home; she had become curious about what the three got up to together. Vera Trevor had a round face, a freckled neck and a look of beaming good-naturedness. Her hair was an unruly mysterious pile, curly, high, quivering with a second nervous life above her. She had never really managed to befriend Stella Keene—it helped a little now to know that she was actually ill, and not just rejecting the country-hand-of-friendship—but had always liked her daughter, ever since she had pulled her, slippery and full of life, from her mother's body. Vera Trevor wished secretly that she could adopt Perdita—poor mite, her father a cold fish, her mother off with the fairies, and stuck here, with nothing much, not even a doll, in this god-awful shack. When Mrs. Trevor pulled back the flyscreen to find Billy, Mary and Perdita looked up to see her shocked expression. It had been at least two years since she had entered the shack and she found it crammed now with books and festooned with images of war. Poor mite, she thought again. Two crazy parents.

"Where's Billy?" she asked, for something to say, and both girls simultaneously turned and directed with their chins, Aboriginal style, out the window to the left. *Poor mite. Like a blackfella.*

For those who do not read, for whom reading is not part of the texture of knowing, the gorgeous complication, the luxurious interiority, the thrilling extrapolation from black marks to alternative reals; for those who might not understand what it is to collaborate in making a world, or building a thought, or consolidating, line by line, the salvage of something long gone; for those bereft, that is, and booklessly broke, those word-deprived, craving, caught in dull time, it will seem odd that two girls, with not much to do, spend a few hours of each day hidden in the valleys of pages. Proxy lives, new imaginings, precious understandings.

When Mrs. Trevor appeared in the doorway, Perdita and Mary were both reading. Both were otherworldly and somewhere else. It startled them, seeing Mrs. Trevor, and she too was startled. They could see a kind of flinch in her body and her high hair quaking. Perdita was a hundred or so pages into *David Copperfield*; Mary was reading a book on the life of Captain Cook. They were ensconced, happy.

After their girlhoods have been lost forever and Perdita's spoken words turned to a forced, gluey halting, both remembered how easy it had been to dwell there, side by side, together and separate, in such safe, quiet pages. In the granular light of the shack, penetrated more by shadow than by light, they sat quietly together reading, their heads flared open like parasols, open and inclining with sisterly ease.

Mrs. Trevor had brought them a cake to share. It was a chocolate cake, frosted with thick brown icing. Perdita sprang forward and clasped Mrs. Trevor around the neck, kissing her loudly, burying her face in her curls, and Vera felt for a moment that she might cry, here and now, in this mean little shack with its mad decorations. Some private thought released—that she had always wanted a daughter, that she had tried, and tried, and then Billy came, decisively, to end her trying. That evening she would tell her husband that maybe the Government should know, a little girl like that, stuck in the back of nowhere, with no mother to watch over her: it shouldn't be allowed. She needed proper looking after. A mother. A real mother.

For now, they found Billy and sat together and shared the cake. Mrs. Trevor sliced it in generous portions, pleased to see the three faces looking so grateful, and so hungry for what, in loving kindness, she had baked and brought. She watched the three of them eat; Billy, her favourite son, despite the fact that he was slow, ate with a kind of fastidious care, his teary gaze fixed resolutely on the floor. Vera could tell he was afraid of the newspaper images tacked to the wall because he began to flap his hands in agitation whenever he caught sight of them. Mary ate, Mrs. Trevor thought, just like a native, stuffing it in as if afraid it would disappear before she claimed it, no table manners, really, not even from the convent; and Perdita, well, Perdita, she was just normal, Vera thought, just a normal little girl, affectionate, sweet, pretty in her own speckled way, and stuck in the wrong bloody place with the wrong bloody parents.

When all had eaten their fill Vera Trevor left, taking Billy with her. There was something about the shack that chilled and disturbed her, something murky, unnatural, a zone of the *abnormal*. She told Perdita to visit whenever she liked, but felt ill at ease, and a little cowardly, leaving her behind. When she turned to look back, Mary and Perdita had already re-entered the shack, not even waiting long enough for a wave.

*

On the same day that Mrs. Trevor visited Perdita with the chocolate cake, Mandjabari, from the camp, came to the shack to visit Mary. Perdita had noticed, with a little jealousy, how fond they were of each other. She had seen Mary join her, from time to time, in the creek-bed, she had seen their muffled conversations in the patchy shade of acacia and their shy, solicitous waves to each other. Mandjabari stood behind the screen door, not even touching it, but seeming like a figure behind a veil, pencilled in and receding. Her presence was formal, somehow, but unassuming, faint. She rocked a little on her heels, so that the shape she made shifted. Mary whispered something in Language, then turned to Perdita.

"Come, we're going out."

Perdita grabbed her hat hanging from the bent nail beside the doorway and followed without question. They went first to the creek-bed to share a billy of tea. The men were all away somewhere, old man Dauwarrngu and the others, so it was just the women and children sitting together in a circle around the fire. The tea was sweet and black and tasted gritty and smoky, and Perdita, who was used to canned condensed milk in her tea, found it undrinkable. Mary said something to the others in Language. An old woman raised her withered breast and pointed her nipple at Perdita, gently making fun of her, and everyone laughed. Perdita looked at Mary and saw her smiling back. Light struck the side of her face so that her smile seemed radiant. She wanted, for Mary's sake, to drink the terrible tea. She wanted to show that she was part of the group. Not to be subtracted, as she was in her parents' presence. Perdita sipped the bitter tea. She felt proud of herself.

It was mid-afternoon, a time of slanting shadows and hot sticky stillness. Perdita, with Mary holding her hand, followed the small band of women as they headed slowly into the bush. Each took turns carrying a tousled-haired girl, about three, and it seemed to Perdita, especially when it was her turn carrying the bony child, that they walked for miles and miles, always in the same direction. They had their backs to the sun and their long shadows were swaying and melding, an all-dark community, proceeding before them.

When they came to an area of escarpment, just before a plain, the women became quiet and began to separate out, searching for food. It was uneven rocky country, hard walking country. Perdita found nothing. She saw the figures around her, moving outlined against the indigo sky, squatting, or bent over, or shifting with gentle tread, and felt herself tiny, and insignificant, and unequal to this place. Once she saw at a distance a frilled-neck lizard and made a quick lunge in its direction, but it fled, its membranous neck flaring open transparently, like an alien blossom.

The afternoon dragged. Perdita gave up her hunting and studied ants swarming at her feet. She chipped away at an anthill with a piece of rock, enjoying the crumble. It was Mary, in the end, who was the big success. She captured and killed a red-bellied black snake, whipping it onto a rock, breaking first its back, and then crushing its head with her digging stick.

"Eh!" she called, waving.

It occurred to Perdita only then that Mary was known for her hunting prowess, that at sixteen she was already skilled and admired. Mary allowed Perdita to carry the tail end of the snake. They walked back with the limp creature swinging in a bow between them. It looked, Perdita thought, as if she had caught it too, as if Mary was proclaiming a truly shared glory. When they arrived back at the camp, at sunset, the men had returned and hailed Mary and Perdita together. The girls held the snake up high, not a trophy, but an offering, and not mere food, but evidence of their special connection.

8

As an adult she cannot remember what might have prompted it, but in a rare moment of communication Nicholas decided to tell Perdita about ideas of kin. For Aboriginal people, he said, kin was organisation, the structure of rule, obligation, system, code. He drew a circle and began to divide it into spokes, so that it resembled a cake. In eight segments he wrote the names of "skin" groups, different orders of kin affiliation, then explained to Perdita that opposition and proximity on the wheel determined relationships.

She nodded thoughtfully, barely understanding. She picked at a scab on her knee and brushed it to the floor. Nicholas added that kin would have to be destroyed if Aborigines were to enter the modern world. It made them share everything, he said, so they were always poor and could never accumulate property. It made them think in communal, not individual terms, so that they were always bound to the past, to tribal savagery, not looking forward to the new self that would equip them for twentieth-century Australia. This was one of the chief propositions of his research "hypothesis."

Perdita nodded again, keen to make her father believe she thought his ideas important.

"Mmm," she said gravely, offering an imprecise affirmation. She saw her father's hand hover in a slight tremor above the page he had drawn. It was a dim, muggy day, the air was charged with the possibility of an electrical storm, and Perdita met her father's gaze through his fogged-up spectacles. At this moment he seemed most human, and almost vulnerable: he was asking his young daughter to confirm his ideas. His face was glowing with perspiration, his hair slightly upright with atmospheric energies and currents. How reddish his face was, an Englishman oppressed by the weather, straining to clarify systems and to figure designs. A sudden crack of thunder made them both jump. They could hear the world outside filling with exclamations of power, the verve of pressure, inflation, of air masses moving. They could hear a wind from the west, brimming with physical threat and loaded with sky-lakes of heavy water. Nicholas took his glasses from his face and wiped each lens with scholarly deliberation, then he wiped his shiny forehead with the same handkerchief and turned away. Geckos on the ceiling were clicking madly, incited by the vibrating charge in the air.

Perdita did not know if her father was correct, but what she had gathered was this: that in the culture of the people she knew there were multiple uncles and aunts, multiple brothers and sisters, and that the cake-shape enabled everyone to know how to behave and whom they should marry. When she asked Mary about this, she learned that she—Perdita—had been given a skin group: since Mary had a designated daughterly role in relation to Mandjabari, Perdita was included as a sister. Mary told her matter-of-factly, thinking it a casual disclosure, but Perdita was both surprised and delighted. She knew herself suddenly implicated in a wider pattern, where there would always be someone, somewhere, to know of and look after her; and she knew too of the formal recognition of her love for Mary, her sister. The Trevors, she discovered, did not have a skin group, but this was when Perdita decided once and for all that Billy was her brother, just as she had intimated to the cook, that day, talking about her family in the Continental Hotel.

Perdita examined her skin. It was freckled and pale, the

mark of her foreignness in this place, the mark of implicit defi-
ciency. She wanted so much to be dark. When she placed her
forearm alongside Mary's she saw herself the bright negative of
a surer presence. Mary teased and humoured her.

"No worries," she said. "Stay this place long enough and
you'll maybe turn blackfella. Maybe marry a blackfella too and
have blackfella babies."

Mary leaned forward and kissed her cheek.

"No worries," she said again.

One night Mary announced that sometimes she thought of
Annie McCaughie as another sister: Annie, who had died of
measles or diphtheria, Annie forever a little girl, and With Our
Gentle Lord, and Resting in Peace. She had worn Annie's
clothes, inherited her book, carried about her neck the dead
girl's cross on a chain—until, that was, someone at the orphanage stole it—and had *read the same words*. Mary had a theory
that when people read the same words they were imperceptibly
knitted; that there were touchings not of the skin, and appari-
tional convergences. Some kind of spirit inhered in words that
one might enter and engage with; there were transactions, com-
minglings, adjacencies of mind and of sense. Mary's version was
simpler, of course, but for years later Perdita considered how
this superstition worked; Mary extended to written words the
forms of community she longed to express, just as, in their generosity, the creek people had bestowed on Perdita a relation-
ship of skin. By this reasoning, too, David Copperfield was part
of her and Captain Cook was part of Mary; and even in the
world-weariness that reading sometimes induces, they
absorbed irresistibly, naïvely, elements of the lives they imagined. A kind of family without limits. Occult relations.

*

One month before Christmas Nicholas collected Stella from

the hospital and brought her home. She had been gone six months, some of which time was spent in the convent. Nicholas also brought a pile of newspapers, a few many weeks old, and packages of books. A photograph of Winston Churchill appeared with the other images on the wall, so the return of Stella was marked iconographically by the introduction of this man— his square baby-face, his obstinate glare, his rude pugnacity. Stella looked about herself meekly, as though she had mislaid something important. She spoke in a quieter voice and her skin had the quality of a porous fossil, sallow, chalky, more contracted to the bone, more like the old woman she had prematurely become. Her hair was grey. She was fifty-two years old. Perdita was filled with affection when she saw her mother, so reduced and unfamiliar. In the histories of mothers and daughters there are no doubt everywhere these instances of sudden feeling, insurgent, after times of alienation. Perdita rushed forward and embraced her, clasping her around the waist, pushing her face into her mother's thin bony chest, but was aware that her embrace had no reply: Stella stood like a statue, her arms at her sides.

Mary stepped forward and simply took Stella's hand.

"Come," said Mary. She led Stella to the table, sat her down, and gave her a cup of tea. "Drink," she instructed. "Be careful. Hot."

In the morning Perdita saw that Stella's feet looked tiny, childlike, beneath the lacy white hem of her threadbare nightgown.

*

I have never discovered what treatment my mother received, or why, each time, her absences were so long. Whatever electrochemical disturbance seized her in this way, whatever awry synapses or deficient serotonin, she never spoke to me of her condition, or the periods in which she simply left. By the time I was old enough to ask her, she was not interested in replying, and had already begun, in any case, to enter the honeycomb of dementia, the looped craters under-arching what might have been a memory, the brownish corridors to nowhere, the frail struts of something that had once been dense pillars of identity.

I remember watching her lift, with finger and thumb, the corner of an old newspaper, look up distractedly, and say, "Still. The war." Nicholas had promised her we would return to England when the war was over, and perhaps it was now just another slumberous waiting, another unreal suspension, stretched in a duration no clock would show, and not quite persuasive enough to cause her to worry about her family back home. She held up the corner of the newspaper for what seemed ages, frozen by a story, perhaps, or an obscure foreign detail that summarised this or that victory or defeat, or something that reminded her of the holiday she had taken once with Mrs. Whiticombe, when they had crossed the Channel on a ferry, still more or less young, and witnessed for themselves the comfortable exoticism of Belgium and France.

Stella seemed at first unaware of the elapse of time. She was incurious about me, and about Mary, she had not followed the war, she had not read her sister's letters. Only when she noticed, one morning, that I was wearing a dress stretched across the chest and too tight under the arms did she acknowledge that I had grown, that my body was changing, and that, implicitly, time had passed. This returned Stella to sewing, which I now believe was therapeutic. She sewed new dresses for each of us, neat, practical garments.

Once, having miscalculated and ordered too much fabric, she, Mary and I all ended up with dresses of the same rose print, a tent-like shift we each wore, looking like the jovial pink members of a singing club or an English gardening group, uniformed for a whimsy. It reminded her, Stella said, of Martha, Sal and Daff, years ago, who all wore the same dress, comically alike. And as she said this I remembered Sal and Daff in the same sky blue, I remembered one of them holding me, I remembered one of them whispering, and was overcome by a sadness so profound I wondered for the first time if I would become my mother, if I would be this kind of unhappy woman, coiled around emptiness, falling hopelessly silent like a pearl shell at the bottom of the ocean. A crowd trampling through St. Pancras, eddying with their parcels and packages and important bags, calling out, quarrelling, raising their arms for attention, an anonymous crowd, carrying anguish of all kinds, each burdened continuously just by being alive, this population of the head scared and alarmed me; this population was like a threat, like an inheritance of evil I might one day discover.

Sal and Daff linger still, implying something unspeakable. When Stella mentioned their names I dreamed about them the same night, a double woman, seancing them back into being so that I could recover them, if only fleetingly, and as co-joined figments, as distant love-objects, as alternative mothers.

*

Perdita and her family celebrated Christmas that year with Mary still living in the shack. Though her role was undefined, no one seemed to think that she should leave. She cooked more often, and kept Stella company, reading to her as she sewed, as Stella had once read to Mrs. Whiticombe, watching her hands, fingers long and held apart like a pianist, relaxed on the edge of a lavender bedspread. It may have been the idea that she had a servant that pacified Stella—who had always believed that she was misplaced in class—and Perdita, self-interested, enjoyed this small restful period, marked by

Mary's voice and her mother's subsidence into something like peace.

On Christmas Day, however, there was altercation. At first, Stella appeared voluble and happy. Mary, Stella and Perdita each wore their rose-print dresses (Stella's surmounted, unseasonably, by her black Spanish shawl), and her sense of festivity was flamboyant and infectious. During the morning Nicholas smoked alone outside; Perdita could see him through the gauzy window fiddling with strings of tobacco, filling his pipe with his thumb and gazing with unfocused intensity into the far distance; then she could smell the pipe smoke thinly dispersing, its bitter brown spread. But inside, Stella buzzed in a tizzy around the room, placing wildflowers here and there on stacks of books, checking the large chicken roasting slowly in the oven. There were no gifts, but the meal was genial enough—Nicholas and Stella were civil to each other, Perdita and Mary exchanged shy smiles, all enjoyed the treat of roast chicken and salty potatoes, glistening in a golden oily pyramid before them. It might have been a happy family sitting there, sated and complacent.

After the meal, Stella began pouring herself more and more sweet sherry. Her hand grew trembly and her talk erratic. She decided that she would perform, as a Christmas treat, Act Five of *Othello*. Nicholas rolled his eyes to the ceiling, expressing his contempt for the performance before it commenced. He leaned back with his glass, disengaging.

Stella began at the point in the drama when Othello enters Desdemona's bedchamber. She had long ago told Perdita the details of the plot: the black Moor of Venice is enraged with jealousy, goaded by evil Iago to suspect his wife's infidelity. He smothers her (*"Down, strumpet"*), discovers his error, then stabs himself dramatically. It had always seemed to Perdita a more vicious version of *The Winter's Tale*, all waste and fury, all havoc and murderous idiocy, with no one saved. They were still seated at the table, the ruins of their meal uncleared before them, and Stella stood a few feet away reciting the bedchamber scene, modulating her voice between Desdemona and Othello (smothering her even before she can pray!). When she was Othello she wound the shawl, turban-like, around her head, in order to make herself hooded and black, and she spoke in a gruff, stentorian tone.

Stella's time in hospital had not decreased her Shakespearean recall. With surprising facility, she played out the debate between the good Emilia, Desdemona's friend, and Othello just after Desdemona's death. She recited, word-perfect, Othello's long self-justification, his long self-revelation, his long self-indictment. She remembered the scene in which Iago stabs Emilia (his wife), trying to silence her. Emilia protests:

> *"Twill out," twill out. I peace.*
> *No, I will speak as liberal as the north:*
> *Let heaven and men and devils, let them all,*
> *All, all, cry shame against me, yet I will speak.*

Stella's voice rose higher and higher, inordinate and tough. And by the time she had arrived at Othello's closing speech, she was overwrought, shrill, full of her own vehemence. Wrapped in the Spanish shawl, tangled in difficult feelings, she twisted herself into misery before she mimed her own stabbing and collapsed on the floor:

> *I pray you, in your letters,*
> *When you shall these unlucky deeds relate;*
> *Speak of me as I am; nothing extenuate . . .*

Nicholas had also been overindulging. Sherry adorned his white shirt-front in a colourful stain, a trail of roses not unlike those decorating the dresses they wore. At this point, when Stella was folded into herself as the great tragic Moor, "*who loved not wisely, but too well,*" he let out a deep, derisive laugh. Stella unfolded from the floor and lifted up silently, her speech unfinished. She had tears in her eyes and was still ensnared in the moment of Othello's slow death.

Without warning Stella lurched sideways and in delirious fervour began to strip the newspaper cuttings from the walls, tearing them as she went, furiously ripping the paper, spraying the room with black-and-white newspaper confetti. When she reached Winston Churchill she crushed his face in one grasp and hurled him at Nicholas.

Perdita and Mary were both motionless with fear. They did not even see the moment that Nicholas rose. He had hit Stella before they knew, sending her flying backwards so that she toppled a stack of books. When Mary rose to protest, Nicholas also struck her, but though she wavered and was hurt, she did not fall. She stood before him in staunch, smarting accusation, so that he became self-conscious, or perhaps even ashamed.

But no apology was offered. Nothing was said.

Nicholas turned and strode from the room, banging the fly-screen door behind him.

Perdita felt once again the sting of her own cowardice, the way she had become a mute witness, a child whose limits defined her. On the floor before her, Stella was lying still, curled inwards, her nose a bloody mess, the Spanish shawl—*her* Spanish shawl, only for distinctive occasions, only for rare Shakespearean splendour—cast off, tossed negligently, like a black dead thing. There was heavy breathing and soft weeping and the tumultuous event settling down. There was no past and no future, just this painful arrest, in which impulse stilled and sensation flickered into prominence. There was ebbing, slack release. It was Perdita who performed the low, soft weeping. It was Perdita's role to conclude *Othello*, to lament for fierce, corruptible men, to mourn the despicable intensities that might enter and shatter a family.

Outside a murder of crows cawed, their voices harsh. It was still Christmas Day. On 29 and 30 December that year—the war-time year of 1940—a massive German air raid attacked and bombed London, killing, among others, both Stella's parents and her younger sister, Iris, a spinster, who was still living at home. Stella did not find out about their deaths until early 1942. So many injuries in the world, so many violations.

9.

It was a hot day, the air lolling and billowy, stirring from the east. Nicholas had been gone, with Mr. Trevor, for almost four days, and the house relaxed into a comfortable, easy pattern. In the front room, shadowed by books, Mary was relieving Stella of lack of purpose by teaching her the rules of poker. The suits, the scorings, the calculated value of a hand. She laid out the suits on the kitchen table, lining up the black with the black and the red with the red, and forming the hierarchical domains of the look-alike monarchs. Stella was instantly captivated. There was an order here, and fierce competition. She loved at once the sequential feel of the shuffle, and the swift distribution of slippery cards, flung like flying saucers from a flick of the wrist. She loved the fan shape as she held the cards and decided which to retain and which to dispose of, and the slapping of a card on the table, and the grabbing up of a replacement. Mary did not, Perdita noticed, teach Stella how to cheat, and every now and then she saw her mother beaten, sitting forward in her chair looking addled and glum, with Mary, poker-faced, disclosing not a thing. They tried not to catch each other's glance; it was another understanding they shared, and spoke of in the darkness.

Billy was the most skilled player of the group. At each game he bent over his cards with exacting attention; he hated to be distracted or touched, and focused only on the glossy rectangles sprayed before him, their exchanges, their values, their feasible realignments. His ginger head was bent in concentration; his freckled hands flashed out, releasing and gaining cards. When he smiled, it was wonderful. His crooked teeth were endearing. Even Stella was charmed.

Between the four of them they spent many hours at cards, and for a brief period at the beginning of 1941, it was a rational system surrounding them all, an inconsequential orderliness, reassuring and trite. Newspaper cuttings had begun reappearing on the walls. Once Perdita glanced sideways during a game and began to read what was before her. The Germans and Italians had engaged in conflict with the Greeks, and British, Australian and New Zealand forces had been dispatched from Egypt. Perdita imagined armies in the night, marching orders, columns of uniformed, look-alike men. At once she knew with startling clarity, like a punch in the ribs, one of the terrible, unassimilable anomalies of this world: that there is always war somewhere and peace somewhere else, that there are people dying and—*at the same time*—there are people playing cards, sipping, as they do, from cups of sweetened tea, preoccupied only by the pleasures and vexations of a cardboard figure.

It was April and Perdita will remember all her life the moment she understood this rupture in the texture of life. She was ten years old. She glanced up, pleased with two Aces and the possibility of a third, and saw in a newspaper cut-out the vague grey shape of a soldier, stooping, beaten, slumped around his rifle. His face was obscured in shadow but his posture was eloquently distressed. The image was by then already a little tattered—it had been on the wall for two weeks at least—but it seemed suddenly to address her. This was a man whose job it was to kill, and somewhere, behind the image, were the corpses he had made, post-mortally transforming to grotesque blue jellies, and those too, perhaps, of some of his comrades, indistinctive in the banal democracy of death. And the day after the photograph he would again kill or be killed. He would revive from slumped exhaustion and return to his job. Perdita had yet to see the archives of victims that would appear only after the war ended, but this was enough. She thought to herself: *I am ten years old, there is a world war going on, I am playing cards.* And there the moment stopped.

The lanky stockman, Willie, appeared at the screen door and without opening it announced that Nicholas had fallen from a horse. Nothing serious, but he would spend one or two nights in the hospital in Broome while a doctor checked and bandaged his ribs. Stella smiled. She looked down at her cards. There was silent celebration. Perdita knew then her second significant revelation: *tyranny, and release from tyranny, occur everywhere, and in every scale.*

*

The wind rose higher, the barometric pressure fell. There was something ominous in the air, a swelling and tumbling. At first Stella noticed the heaviness about her, but then heard that the birds had gone quiet, or had fled, or altogether disappeared. Small stirrings occurred, a circular sweep of dried leaves, the uplift of sand in a reddish spiral. It took her only seconds to realise that a cyclone was approaching. Stella called Mary and Perdita inside, and they waited there, listening to the world of inanimate things begin to rouse and animate. Outside rain began to fall, sweetening the air, then there was the slightest tremble to the world around them. The table seemed to move, the chair slightly to shift. Rain-beat on the roof became heavier and heavier, and with the rain sound came a gradually increasing roar. All at once, the sky was falling in. All at once, the sound was like the noise of St. Pancras Station—echoing and inhuman, hugely threatening.

Stella fell to the floor and began to cry. Perdita saw Mary bend and clasp her mother close, then wipe the tears from her face with the open palm of her hand.

As though in mysterious repetition, someone appeared, wet and glistening, at the flyscreen door. It was a shape, at first, as Mandjabari had been that day, patiently entreating Mary to join her; as Willie has been when he announced Nicholas's accident. But Perdita saw when the screen opened that it was not Mandjabari but Kurnti, the man who had been in chains, the man she had waved to, a year ago now, as he laboured outside the Continental Hotel. Stella saw him enter and let out a little scream, but Perdita calmed her.

"Kurnti," she said. "It's Kurnti, come to save us."

She was not sure why he had suddenly appeared, or why she had designated him a saviour. But now the noise of the storm was booming and the walls were shuddering, as if the shack was a motor engine, turned over and starting up; and it seemed just one more out-of-the-ordinary event, this man's black face, made silver with rain-slick, asking in a shout if her mother was all right, squatting in front of them, his knobbly knees akimbo, with a look of earnest enquiry and concern.

Perdita saw bits of the war clippings tear and fly off the walls and a china cup on the table shake to the edge, and fall to the floor with a disintegrating smash. Books opened their covers and pages turned by themselves. A stack of cards near where the teacup had stood began flipping upwards, one by one, so that hearts, clubs, diamonds and spades went spinning, fifty-two of them, throughout the room. Perdita observed this activity with a kind of joy: the images dispatched, flipping into the wind, the turning of pages, the ghostly reading.

Kurnti ran into the bedroom and, above the noise, called on the others to follow. He heaved the double mattress off the bed and held it up like a roof; they all lay on their bellies and he lowered it around them, before sliding under himself. So there they were, together waiting for the cyclone to pass.

As quickly as it had begun, everything quietened. The moist air stilled. Perdita could hear playing cards flutter and settle in the other room, susurrations of paper, curtains, feather-sounds, sighs. She held her breath. They waited in silence. It was stifling under the heavy mattress, a choking heat, but Kurnti said simply: "Wait; comin' back."

The other side of the storm seemed more uproarious and violent. Rain poured as if from a massive funnel above them; there was again the shaking of walls and the railway roar. A waterfall scrim appeared at the window. Stella began to chant:

> *Blow, winds, and crack your cheeks! rage! blow!*
> *You cataracts and hurricanes, spout*
> *Till you have drenched our steeples, drowned the cocks!*

She had entered a trance of intensity. Her voice, challenging the heavens, was deep and strained.

> *You sulphurous and thought-executing fires,*
> *Vaunt-couriers to oak-cleaving thunderbolts,*
> *Singe my white head! And thou, all-shaking thunder,*
> *Strike flat the thick rotundity of the world!*

Perdita recognised the speech as one from *King Lear*. She hated the idea that her mother might boost or encourage the storm by her fanatical invocation. But then Stella ceased her recitation and resumed her anxious crying. Perdita could feel her mother's body heave in intermittent sobs, and sensed her general fear, and her wish to die. There was a crack like gunfire. A sheet of iron lifted from the roof and spun away. The banging of other sheets loosening their nails set a rough tattoo and seemed suddenly louder. The sky was let in and the room was gusty and wet. Leaves and bits of stick whirled through the air; a tiger snake was washed from a recess beneath the roof and hung suspended above them, swaying and twirling like a party streamer, its body conducting a white line of water.

When it was over they pushed back the mattress and rose to their feet.

Kurnti smiled. "Bloody good one, eh?" He rose, looked around. "Safe now. C'mon."

Perdita embraced Kurnti and thanked him. She was thanking him for his smiling silver-slick face; she was thanking him for coming to the shack no one else cared about; she was thanking him for protecting her from her mother's black-magical speech—a world of thought-executing fires and all-shaking thunder, a world in which a cyclone might be commanded, by rough magic, to flatten the shape of the earth. She turned and saw that Mary was holding Stella. Mary was brushing back hair from her face as one does for a child. Her palm rested on Stella's forehead, as if testing for hurt, or a fever.

Mary looked directly at Perdita and repeated Kurnti's words: "Safe now. C'mon."

The pure notes of a butcher bird rang out in the air.

"'Im one Maban butcher bird," Kurnti declared, touching his ear to make them listen.

"Magic fella," Mary whispered.

The notes scaled upwards; Mary nodded at Perdita.

"Safe now."

Together they walked outside and saw the gleaming world, everything bright but wrecked, everything washed clean but destroyed. A kerosene tin bucket was caught high in the branches of a bloodwood. Sticks and iron fragments lay all about. Inside things were outside, clothing, images. How easily the look of the world reversed; how easily a squall, spraying warm rain and blowing like crazy, might re-order and trouble ordinary objects. Stella saw a playing card floating in the red, streaming mud at her feet and bent to retrieve it.

"The cards," she said, through her tears. "We must find the cards."

Perdita watched her mother scrabble on all fours in the

disorder of the departed storm. She was filmy in the grey light, her face pale and possessed. Horatio had appeared from nowhere and was sniffing the ground with excitement, his tail a wild flag. In the distance there was a fan of light, where the sun had just hidden. There were shapes, tumbling like ocean, and turmoil retreating. There were lightning flashes in the sky, long and sharp as knives.

*

In the life of every child there are times in which the symbolic gains more weight and magnitude, when childish things, and their comforts, are put away, and there form the intuitions and understandings that ground the later adult. These are known only in retrospect, just as the gist of any tragedy is apparent only at its conclusion. The meaning of one's parents -the remote father, the unstable mother—is likewise discovered when they cease to have authority over us, in death, or in the mind's demented retreat, or in the distances we manage to create as adults. But at seven, or eight, or nine years old, we may nevertheless glimpse them, sense in a hunch what will later unfold, know in the briefest presentiment their true specificity, and the claims they will have on us. When I saw my mother searching for the cards, disregarding me, and the busted house, and the storm-wrack all around, when I guessed she was acting out Lear tormented, believing herself infirm, weak and despised, I realised in a wave of pity that I was stronger than she and would be called upon some day to act my part and protect her. Her wet hair hung in rats' tails beside her face, her thin cotton dress was spattered with red mud, she was bedraggled and lost. And she was searching in desperation, as if she had misplaced her own heart.

We never recovered the entire pack of cards. There were forty-two when at last we cleaned and counted them. The search in the mud made Stella distraught. At last she rose up and wrung out the hem of her dress. The sense in each of us assembled—Mary, Kurnti and I—was of a woman blasted hollow by what she could not understand.

*

When my father returned, his torso bandaged, I realised that I resented him. Mary flinched at his presence. Stella withdrew. Unmanned by his accident, Nicholas snarled at us all, and demonstrated his capacity for careless brutality. Once he spilled his fiery pipe on Mary's bare arm, burning a scarlet hole the size of a two-shilling piece. As she brushed away the hot tobacco, she refused to cry.

Warily, we watched him and moved out of his way. A menacing possibility had entered our lives. We feared him, waiting as one waits for the arrival of a cyclone, cringing, cautious, to see what destruction it will leave, to see what it is that converts a home to a ruin.

PART THREE

MALCOLM: Let us seek out some desolate shade,
and there Weep our sad bosoms empty.

Macbeth, IV iii

10

T his time it was Mary, not Stella, they took away.
The day unveils itself in partial scenes and stages, as if a memory-camera is fixed, and cannot swing around to envision the entire room or every one of the players. From this angle Mary stands in her hydrangea-blue dress, stained purple and lurid with Nicholas's blood; the knife is close by; she looks utterly guilty. It is early afternoon and the air is flame-tinted and warm, streaming with motes, heavy now with the gravity of death descending, of crime, of consequences, of what will soon break open. Mary begins to cry. She is in shock and both sure and unsure of what has occurred. Her body quakes. Perdita steps forward to comfort her. The two girls hold hands and cry together. If we were to zoom in we would see that their faces look the same: with the expression of distress they have indeed become sisters. In the background are stacks of books, lined all around the walls, and newspaper cuttings of war stories, photographs and maps. This is a complicated scene; there is almost too much to take in.

When the two policemen from Broome arrive, summoned by Mr. Trevor, they will discover what appears to them a madman's shack. What kind of bloke would have this many books in the bush? What idiot would pin war images where a little girl was sleeping? In the pink light of twilight they will examine the body of Nicholas Keene, left where he fell, his back and neck pierced crudely and roughly by a knife.

They will comment on how much blood has seeped away,

how blotchy the skin is, how death comes with such ugliness. They will notice the shrapnel scars on his back and the trousers unbuttoned, slid to his ankles. They will take notes, real notes, like the blokes in the city, pleased to have a genuine murder to deal with, something crimson and scandalous they can tell their mates about later on.

In the air is a criminal stench of blood. They breathe it in. They fill themselves. As night falls and the sense of drama begins to shift, the policemen will question the little white girl, who says virtually nothing, and seems to have trouble forming words in her mouth. Then they question the older black girl, who has confessed, anyway, and the surprisingly self-composed wife, who talks clearly and succinctly about what has occurred. It is clear that the black girl, Mary, has been raped. Bruises are already appearing on her thighs and at her neck. Mrs. Trevor confirms that she's heard rumours about Nicholas Keene and native girls: she hadn't believed it at first and had once sent away a bloody good cook, her best cook ever, because she thought she was lying about Nicholas Keene, who had not long arrived, and had a baby and wife, who seemed educated and well-spoken and was rather handsome, in fact. Didn't seem the sort, not at all, she added.

The policemen roll the body onto an oily canvas sheet, tie each end with a rope, and lift it between them, sharing the weight, onto the back of their ute. They wipe their hands on their trousers before shaking hands with Mr. Trevor, who nods, and looks serious, but is also grimly enjoying this event and its tellable possibilities. He touches the brim of his hat as he says goodbye.

Light from a kerosene lamp streams out of the open door of the shack: everyone present notices how unevenly it wavers, noting that the fuel is low, and they will soon be left in darkness. Large moths are nevertheless hitting against the wire of the door, drinking in what light there is. The girl Mary is with the policemen: she is quiet and compliant. She sits between them in the front seat for the long ride into the darkness. The little white girl watches as they drive away. In the rear-view mirror they can see her child-shape waving, as if she has just had a visitor, and not a murder, to deal with.

Mary does not look back. Mary looks into the night, tunnelled by headlights that catch at animal eyes, ruby glints, vague darting things, and the trunks of trees that appear to swerve, again and again, into deadly near-collision.

*

Time looped back and replayed. Mary was driven away into the darkness and Perdita vigorously waved, as if waving still meant something. She saw the twin chutes of the headlights fork out into the night, swing left, illuminate a boab, and then recentre. Behind her, inside, Perdita could hear Mr. and Mrs. Trevor talking to Stella, telling her to gather some things, to come and stay for the night. Billy was with them, clutching at his mother's arm to stop his own rising up and flapping, to still his large, inexpressible shock. When Perdita re-entered the shack she saw her mother stepping around the glossy black stain that had been her father's life. She felt a numbing tingle in her body and a clogging in her mouth.

Stella glanced at her daughter and said simply: "Let's go."

There was no discussion of what had occurred in that room; no words would explain or commemorate between them, or allow either to say what swelled horribly within their hearts. Stella put her index finger to her mouth in a gesture of stern silencing, "Shh!" She took Perdita's hand and almost dragged her away.

That night Billy visited Perdita as she lay, unable to sleep, on the thin prickly mattress placed on the veranda of the Trevors' house. Mrs. Trevor had tucked her in clean sheets, given her a cup of warm powdered milk, even kissed her gently on the cheek as her own mother had never done. But then she was left alone with the night sounds: scratches, creaks, the breathy sob of the wind. A three-quarter moon was rising in the sky. Everything was softening, achieving a cloak of weak light. The trees were pale; the clouds above carried a pearly, irregular fringe. For the first time Perdita thought about the existence of ghosts and became afraid. He might be there now, distending into phantasmic, airy shapes, long-fingered, eyeless, yawning and strange, his back and neck gaping open where the knife had been. He might be floating between the book-stacks, wreathing around her bed, passing restlessly in and out of the room where last night he was alive and sleeping.

When Billy crept to her bed, Perdita let him in. He made whimpering sounds. He might also have been afraid. They lay together clutching, and it was then that Perdita knew that Billy had seen everything, and would know for always, for ever and ever, know in the pools of his unblinking, watery grey eyes what role each had played and what had occurred. Perdita liked the firm feel of Billy's body, so warm and solid and unghostly against hers. When she tried to speak to him—even though he could not hear—she found herself stuttering. Something fretful and uncommon pestered her tongue, some mischief was there, some remnant of the day. Perdita did not panic; she assumed it would pass.

Billy rose and went to piss from the edge of the veranda. He was unselfconscious, leaning his hips forward, tilting his belly, and Perdita saw the arc of his water shine in the moonlight. But when he returned to the bed Perdita reached down to feel his body and discovered he had his hands crossed over his private parts. She lifted them away and rested her own hand there, to comfort him, to show that she understood. From inside the house, very faintly, Perdita heard her mother's voice:

Avaunt! and quit my sight! Let the earth hide thee!
Thy bones are marrowless, thy blood is cold;
Thou hast no speculation in those eyes
Which thou dost glare with!

Perdita remembered the speech. It was Macbeth, with
bulging vision, seeing slain Banquo's ghost. Yet Stella did not
sound afraid or alarmed, or as if she had actually seen
Nicholas's ghost; she sounded simply as if she was reciting to
calm herself to sleep, to hear in measured language what was
otherwise fearsome, night-shrieking and dire.

Billy lifted his face as if he too had heard the speech.
Perhaps he too was thinking about ghosts, *"prisoners of the
wind."* In the semi-darkness Billy appeared even stranger than
usual: his eyes were saucers, his hair copper wire, his features
stylised by the fluid moonlight they both seemed to float in.

*

Vera Trevor could not persuade her Aboriginal domestic
help to clean up the blood in the Keenes' shack. Downright
refused, she said. No way, no way. No amount of threat or per-
suasion changed their minds. Debil-debil there, they told her.
But she couldn't imagine what devils they were referring to,
now that Nicholas's body was gone, taken away for a coroner's
report, and Mary locked up. She and Stella had to do the job
themselves. They took buckets and mops and ammonia cleaning powder, and on their knees scrubbed away at the mess of
death. With their brushes they formed arm's-length pink-
coloured swirls of foam, then mopped up, and squeezed, and
found beneath them a wooden floor that had not quite forgotten the crime. When Vera realised that the outline of the
bloodstain was ineradicable, she contributed a rag mat to
cover what remained. It was a vivid mat, multicoloured and

rather jolly. Stella was grateful. It was nice, she said. It brightened the place up.

*

The morning was sunny, renewed. It was possible to believe that what had happened was a terrible dream, and that Mary was there, and Nicholas, and the order of things was restored. Yet Perdita found that some trace of the violence remained like congestion in her mouth. When she asked for her breakfast it was already apparent. Something mangled her speech, syllables jammed in her mouth, she could not begin simple words because the consonants would stick. Stella was that morning like a sleepwalker; unresponsive and quiet. She looked up at her daughter, but did not pass comment or express surprise.

Mrs. Trevor leaned across the table and commanded Perdita to open her mouth: she peered in like a dentist, but found no infection or blockage.

"Poor mite," she said, non-committally, giving Perdita's right cheek a little pat with her hand.

But then she went back to eating her toast, offering no further mollycoddle, so that even Perdita did not realise how entrenched the alteration might be. They ate their breakfast in heavy silence. Their gazes did not meet. They were each alone.

Later, in the afternoon, Stella and Mrs. Trevor went to clean the shack. Stella had woken fully by then and seemed sensible and practical in the context of death, just as she had the night before, when the policemen questioned her. Billy and Perdita stayed behind, playing cards on the veranda.

Perdita wondered where Mary was, whether she was in gaol. She imagined her in a windowless room, sitting alone. She imagined Mary's head bent, like a saint, and her dark face prayerful. And she imagined a religious light, a beam of iridescence, flowing from the star of an overhead lamp. She could not bear to think of the Broome gaol, a dour ugly building, hard and forbidding, or of the prisoners she had seen linked by heavy chains, sweating in the sunshine, their faces creased and exhausted and verging on desperation. Perdita needed to convince herself that Mary was somewhere unworldly and safe.

It was after the cleaning that Stella really noticed that Perdita's speech had changed. She told her daughter to pull herself together, to stop being stupid. Perdita sensed at this moment an overwhelming loneliness: Mary gone, her mother angry, no one to talk to. No one to talk to in this incredible, newly warped voice, this juddery, hunchbacked, troublesome voice. What had lodged inside her? What had stuck in her mouth like muck, like vile disturbance? Already resignation was beginning to claim her.

At night they returned together to the shack. Mr. Trevor had been there already and refilled and lit the kerosene lamps. As they walked towards it under the three-quarter moon, Perdita saw from the outside how very small their world was, how frugally they lived. Two rectangular windows shone like animal eyes in the darkness; the shape of the building was crouching, cowered. She felt a rising apprehension at the thought of re-entering the room where her father had bled to death and saw him again, his life ebbing, looking weary and surprised. She wondered if dying people always looked surprised, if death was like that, flabbergasting, and delivered from behind.

Where Nicholas had fallen there was now the oval rag mat, which Perdita had seen before, in the Trevors' house. It was a cheery, a glorious lie, a text of other men's shirts and cast-offs, floral and scrappy fragments, of something that was once worn by Sal and Daff. Perdita stepped onto the mat with a little shudder. There was a smell too, just perceptible, of eucalyptus smoke. She discovered later that the people from the creek had smoked the house. They had dragged smouldering leaves around the room, to clear the contaminating violence of slaughterous thoughts, to release from captivity the unquiet spirit. They had let Nicholas drift away; they had let him be air.

11

When I try to recall those first weeks after my father's death, my memory falters. Burdened as I was by the loss of my fluent speech, other events lessened in importance, or were unremarked. Stella took to wearing her Spanish shawl—this is a reliable image because others, I recall, remarked upon it, taking the extravagance as a sign of genuine mourning. I did not attend the funeral. Children did not then, it seems, so there is no tidy memory of my father encased, flower-covered, eulogised and sealed away, framed in his coffin by the beams of a high church ceiling, like an image in a movie. There was only the body in the canvas and its rough removal, the policemen veering into the night with Mary sitting between them; then darkness, and a plume of dust, settling in the far reaches of the thinning lamplight.

The days were all the same, dull and empty and governed by grief for my father, for Mary, for all that had changed. Stella and I fell into repetitive reading and sewing. Nicholas's newspapers continued to arrive, and we also became rather obsessed with the war, following it with an interest neither of us had expressed, or had been able to express, when it was hitherto, so definitely, Nicholas's pastime.

Stella retained the newspaper cuttings on the wall and added a few of her own. She particularly liked the map, which from the beginning had been filled in to mark the German expansion and which had not been destroyed in her

Christmas-time rage. Event time was war-time. We wanted a reliable history, a large scale detachment.

My father had been killed when the siege of Leningrad began, in September 1941, just before I turned eleven years old. This was during Stalin's scorched earth policy; and it was when Jews were ordered to wear yellow stars. I knew of Odessa, Kharkov, Sevastapol, Rostov. I had been nowhere, seen nothing, never attended school, yet I held in my head a war-time globe, the *"thick rotundity of the world"* composed of cities aflame, armies massing, territories fought over and lost and turned into graveyards. The map on the wall, corpulent Europe, became covered with Stella's tiny drawings of swastikas. At a distance they looked like spiders, swarming across the paper. From my mother I had already received an engrossing and gaudy education; the world at war magnified my national cartoons and my mechanical geography, and gave me a confident, absurd contemporaneity. I was not squeamish or afraid; no details bruised my heart to make me feel anything more profoundly than I had felt the loss of Mary.

The issue of my speech rankled Stella. She seemed to believe that the stutter was an affectation that I had developed to annoy her, or to dramatise my father's death in the very chamber of my mouth. But in truth I simply found it uncontrollable, and was often in tears with the struggle against my own failure, screwing my mouth into contortions so that I might recover what I had always taken for granted.

Other people also responded with distance. Mrs. Trevor certainly seemed to like me less, thinking I was brain-fevered in some way by the shock of the blood and the knife, and even Billy, who had lip-read, to some extent, my communications in the past, now seemed frustrated by the jerky motions of my meaning. My friends who had inhabited the creek-bed, and who had always welcomed my visits, had disappeared. Willie said they had gone north for ceremonies, for dances, for the "sorry-time" of mourning someone in their own community, someone important. There would be rituals for weeks, dancing, grieving. But I believed that they also missed Mary, and had decided to leave.

I longed for Billy's companionship, but he seemed to withdraw. I saw him staring at the sky, as if to read meaning there, or lying with his face on the dirt, compelled by the wriggling life of some tiny creature. In his own anguish, and missing Mary, he became more pathetic and more than usually disassociated. I watched him drag sticks behind him, leaving trails in the sand, and I wanted nothing more than to walk by his side, to hold his restless hands, to still his blubbery lips and dry his eyes each time he broke into sobbing. Mrs. Trevor, under a large hat, watched over Billy. She willed us apart with her troubled gaze. I imagined she might embrace me, or cure my speaking, but she was distant and suspicious, more critical of Stella, and removed from whatever affection she had once held for me.

I watched Horatio nuzzle at Billy as he lay on the ground, trying to rouse him. Even this upset me: another shift in affections. The dog was mine, not his. I called Horatio to my side and hugged him and slapped his cheeks, to show my possession.

As I talked less, Stella began to talk more, to fill up the shack in which she now felt abandoned. Every now and then she harangued at nothing precisely, complaining about her life and her daughter, addressing God, or William Shakespeare, but mostly she filled the silence with monologic ramblings of a kind of theatrical earnestness and stalwart misery. Her misfortunes were many, she said, but when the war was over they would travel to England, they would live with her sister Margaret, they would start anew. She would make a garden, she said, and fill it with clematis and annual bulbs with fat, scented blossoms, and she would sit in a wicker rocking chair in the soft English light, listening to the wireless.

I was filled with wild loneliness, guilt and grief. I thought I would die for all that remained unexpressed. There was a murder of Jews at Kiev on 29 September, as the Germans began their advance on Moscow. We read about it in November. In history books it says that 33,771 people were killed, men, women and children. I remember knowing only that there was a dreadful massacre at this place, and that with indecent, childish misunderstanding, I attached emotionally to the name *Kiev*, thinking that perhaps it was special enough to contain my vast private woe, my sense that some things, after all, were irremediable.

*

When at last she cast off her Spanish shawl, Stella enlisted Mr. Trevor to teach her to drive. Nicholas's Jeep had stood still for weeks, a monument to his sudden disappearance and the rude persistence of objects over people, but one day Stella noticed it and summoned her neighbour. The battery had become flat, the starter motor had seized, the whole machine was about to become sculptural and dead, but Mr. Trevor bent into its belly and tinkered and repaired. When Stella sat behind the wheel and pumped the accelerator, so that the engine churned and rattled into life, Horatio leaped up, exulting, thinking Nicholas had returned. Perdita saw him sprint from behind the shack to welcome her father home. He circled the car several times, sniffing the earth, looking confused, his vigorous tail gradually stilling. Perdita had seen Horatio search for Mary—turning in sad circles where she once slept, lying beneath the tank stand where she liked to sit and read—but realised now that he also missed Nicholas. There was no howling or fuss; like Perdita, the dog moved in a quiet befuddled sorrow. Perdita left the shack and ran to clasp her dog. They sat in the dirt and watched Stella staring ahead behind the wheel, listening to Mr. Trevor's explanation of the pedals of the car, sitting resolutely where Nicholas had once sat.

The first time they drove to Broome to collect stores, Perdita was excited. She loved going into the town and believed too that she would discover what had happened to Mary. Stella at first drove slowly, testing each corrugation of the road, each gravel and sand trap, but when they arrived both she and Perdita felt a sense of release. They booked for one night at the Continental Hotel and Perdita found it reassuringly unchanged.

Perdita shared a room with her mother, much like the one she had earlier stayed in, and saw that it possessed the same shadowy coolness and aura of calm. The twin beds were high and neat, and draped by conical white mosquito nets. The walls were pale green. There were no war images to look at. Sunshine filtered in stripes through the cyclone-proof shutters. There was an electric light, and even a fan. Perdita would have liked to stay there for ever.

When she was an adult she learned that Stella did not pay the bill, but that the hotel manager, knowing her tragedy, did not insist. Everyone, she discovered, knew of the murdered husband and the crazy wife and the little girl who had seen something that made her words seize and stick. In small towns there exist these discreet forms of solidarity. Nicholas Keene was not well liked, "buggered in the head," they said, "a gutless wonder," but his wife, well, she was a pitiful Englishwoman, without a bloody clue, his daughter a lonesome and isolated stray.

Feeling suddenly unburdened, Perdita flung herself on the bed, and absorbed its luxury (the smell of soap powder, once again, the creaseless cover, the listless encompassing of an over-soft mattress); she remembered her father at the bar, slumping over his whisky, and the palm tree mirror with the liquor bottles lined prismatically before it, and the beautiful woman from the bar, crowned by a high dome of hair, who had given her a packet of salted peanuts. She remembered Sis, from Beagle Bay, who worked out the back in the kitchen, and who had treated her with wise, ineffable tenderness. She remembered the image of her large black hands plunging into a sink of dishes, a voice tone, a compassion.

Early in the evening Stella and Perdita went for dinner to the beer garden. They were served barramundi and chips, with a single ring of canned pineapple, startlingly yellow and balanced, in lieu of salad, at the edge of the plate. Perdita was surprised to see how much food existed in the world. She watched the hotel patrons scoff their meals of fish or steak, and down in huge thirsty gulps their frothy beers. At one point she saw Sis emerging from behind a painted lattice frame. Impulsively, without any hint of hesitation or stutter, she called out her name. Sis turned with a small tray, looked around her, puzzled, then saw Perdita and waved. Perdita waved back. It was like receiving an answer to a necessary question. Sis stood for a moment with her tray, just to look at them. She was smaller than Perdita had remembered and was wearing a tentlike dress patterned with orange hibiscus blossoms. Perdita waved again, across the diners, grateful to be so confirmed.

She was not sure, even later in bed, trying to filter her feelings before sleep, why the exchange of waves had so moved and impressed her. Perhaps, since everyone was disappearing, this sudden reappearance, definite, intense, swathed in large blossoms declarative of festivity, recovered in its sweet sign the possibility of a child she might have been, a child cheerful, unstuttering, a child who has a clean room and a plate of food and knows nothing of death, and nothing of *Kiev*, and who waves—just like that—in spontaneous joy.

In the room that night, under white electric light, Perdita watched Stella slowly undress. It was the first time she had seen her mother's body exposed. Stella was preoccupied and stood naked for a moment, dangling her bra, then flung it sideways onto the bed as she rummaged in her overnight bag for a nightdress. She had a long shapely back and enormous buttocks. The tops of her thighs were dough-like and dimpled. If Perdita had been able to offer a word of love—just as she had called out Sis's name—she would have done so right then. But her fat tongue bulged and her heart pounded: she was afraid she would stutter. She saw the nightdress recovered and lifted above the head. Then the garment coming down, a soft cream sheath, sealing her mother away.

In the morning, in the dazed half-sleep and half-light of just-awakening, Stella whispered in a thick voice across the room to her daughter.

"I had my snow dream again last night."

There was a pause; Perdita waited and heard a slow yawn.

"It's been years, I think, since I've had my snow dream."

Stella was lying inside the cone of the mosquito net. She was masked by white folds, which trembled with the sea breeze that flowed in through the open window. Perdita, barely awake, thought her voice sounded untypically vague and gentle, as if fluttering downwards, as if in slow motion, as if carrying into waking, perhaps, some of the soft qualities of snow.

*

Perdita had developed a rash from lying under the oleander bush in the front yard of the hotel. She held her crimson forearms to her mother and wanted sympathy.

"It's your own fault," said Stella, curtly.

Perdita wanted to see Mary. It was all she wanted. She slung her body into the car, already gritty with their travel, and almost demanded information.

"She's in Perth," Stella said. "At a reformatory school. When she's a bit older, she'll be moved to the prison."

It was enough for now. Mary was away, unreachable. She was no longer in Broome. Perdita looked down at her crimson arms, which had become papery and spotted and itched unbearably. She began softly to cry.

"Cut it out," said her mother, sounding Australian.

On the front of the newspaper between them was balloon-headed Mussolini, saluting the sky. He looked more statue than man; he had a granite angularity. Stella said it was good to see the Italians getting more attention. They were, she claimed, more interesting than Nazis, much more cultured. Cathedrals. Artworks.

"*Duomo*," said Stella emphatically, offering no translation.

When they returned to England, she said, they would have a holiday in Italy, and see Venice, Verona, Mantua and Rome, the Shakespearean cities. She was back in the hard world now, of dictators and deeds to perform, and drove leaning forward over the steering wheel, as if urging the car onward into history.

"Much more interesting."

Perdita longed not for Italy but to move to town. There were pearling luggers floating in the sunlit bay, and a stripe of narrow jetty stretching to meet them. On the shore, close by, were sorting sheds, in which could be glimpsed slender men dressed in sarongs and batik head dresses, sitting cross-legged on piles of shell, examining them, and tossing them into yet new piles. Jewellery, buttons, mother-of-pearl watch faces and ornaments for rich houses: that the town was founded on pearls and pearl shell seemed to Perdita almost impossibly glamorous.

She loved too the people she saw in the streets, Malay, Chinese, Japanese, Filipino, Aboriginal families who lived in houses and were not consigned to stations or missions; they were all much more beautiful than the people she knew. All had black liquid eyes and open faces; they spoke to her with gentleness; they were exotically kind. Perdita also loved the

tin-walled stores owned by Chinese merchants, which were full
of red-papered objects covered in fancy writing, stamped
images of fishes, dragons, circles, cranes. There were noodles
in nest shapes and huge sacks of rice; there were cans of mush-
rooms and fishpaste and cracker-strings of dried chillies. The
objects and smells in the stores—Wings, Tangs—were inexpli-
cably seductive.

Stella bought two Gouldian finches in a temple-shaped
bamboo cage. Perdita was not sure, since the sky was full of
them, why Stella should want two for herself, but was pleased
to witness what was almost frivolity. Stella held them high:
Dromio and Antipholus, she called them. They bounced on
their perches, full of quivering life.

Much of Perdita's knowledge of Broome was derived from
Mary. In town children went to school, and had friends and
played games. There was a Buddhist school for Japanese children (she had seen them sitting outside playing an unfamiliar
board game), a government school for kids like her and for
non-Buddhist Asians, and a Catholic school that had Mass—
whatever that was—where the children, Mary said, learned
stories and mysteries, like those contained in *The Lives of the
Saints*. There was a cinema, and a bakery. Perdita had never
been to the cinema, a small shed, with outdoor seats arrayed in
front of it, and a screen of patched canvas, but she knew that
it must be something marvellous. She knew that the baker had
a drinking problem, that the policeman had a girlfriend as well
as a wife, that there was a woman spirit in the town, a woman
in a red dress, who appeared and disappeared, without reason
or warning. Mary had also told her, somewhat imprecisely, of
the astonishing things men and women got up to together and
Perdita knew there were women who traded their bodies to
men. She wished to see for herself, to stand beside Mary as
they peeped at private moments, to learn truly about the lives
that other people led. The isolation of her destroyed speech

made Perdita aware of the larger isolation in her life; somehow she had not known or realised it before; somehow it had been simply the unexamined condition of things.

They drove first to the stores and the bakery, and then to the convent. Everywhere people turned to look—the English widow, driving a car, bringing her daughter to town; she was a novelty here, and a source of story. Perdita felt particularly conspicuous. She could not reply when addressed and so received pitying looks and insincere pats on the head. It seemed to her that everyone was sorry for her mother (they enquired about her health, made harmless small talk, avoiding mention of the death, as if Nicholas had never existed), but she had the impression they considered her an idiot.

"Terrible business. Terrible," they murmured in collusion.

More condescension awaited at the convent. Perdita was left alone in the foyer where she had first met Mary. A pop-eyed nun with a ruddy complexion gave her a glass of lime cordial, touched her hand lightly and slipped away—not even attempting conversation with the girl whom everyone knew would falter in reply. She was left sitting in a wooden chair so large that it hurt the backs of her bare legs, which dangled like bell ropes without touching the ground. Above her the old-fashioned crucifix still hung; Perdita craned her neck and saw how ugly it now looked. She hated its glossy wood and painted features, the stretched thin body, its ribs apparent, the ludicrous, unbelievable story.

Perdita remembered Mary's body, taller than she, and how she held her arms outstretched, proud of her hunting triumphs, how she slept with her knees drawn up, folded into her own dreaming. It was in this room that Mary had first held her hand. Here, where brazen light showed up the emptiness to things, the apathetic God, the way lives fell apart, the destructive possibilities of any love.

Stella returned with Sister Immaculata and said that there

was no further news of Mary but what they had already gleaned. Sister Immaculata stretched forward and took Perdita's chin with one hand. With the other she prised and stretched back the top and lower lids of the eye that had once been infected.

"Fully healed," she declared.

The nun released Perdita's face. Adults had such pre-emption, took such liberties. Perdita hated the way a hand could reach forward and claim the face; how her mother spat on a handkerchief then held her head tilted and wiped her face clean, dabbing roughly, imperatively. How adults, without asking, made all the decisions. How they claimed to possess all the *big questions*. She was miserable, sullen. Perhaps now, with her newly ruined speech, she would always be someone, a kind of object, whose face was grabbed, who was assumed to have nothing important to say.

Perdita and Stella drove back to the shack in silence, with the finches chirping in the back seat and Mussolini's fat head shuddering between them. Perdita remembered for no reason the stray word *duomo*. Without a clue what it meant, she stored it away in herself, like a buried treasure, its echoic deep sound and its unknown meaning.

12.

At 8 A.M. on 7 December 1941 the Japanese bombed Pearl Harbor, in Hawaii. The newspaper carried a spectacular photograph: the sinking of the USS *Arizona*. Direct hits had sparked its magazine, and the ship exploded in a fireball and sank in five minutes, taking 1300 lives down through a bubbling cauldron of oil. In the photograph the *Arizona* was a ship shape tilted heavenward, covered by smoke and flames. Perdita scanned closely to see the bodies floating in the water, but found none; the image was taken from too far away, from on board, the caption said, the USS *Solace*. It was grainy and imprecise, as befits the dissolving of lives, but too impressively disastrous not to print in the daily paper. There must be many war photographs like this, she thought, too big in scale to include the suffering human, the little man, savagely anointed, his skin blistered with burns, flailing in choppy waters, on the point of drowning. Life was like that. Some deaths were witnessed, some were not; some sobbing victim was going unnoticed, some murdered man fell forward, crumpling onto the floor in an opulent pool of blood, and no one could say what had really happened. This oppressive understanding inhabited Perdita for years; she carried it inside her chest like a brick. The word *Arizona* settled alongside *Kiev*. You could name things, at least. In the absence of a testimonial face, there might at least be a category.

*

To fill what was missing, or to control her bleak sense of intolerable alteration, Perdita took hours-long excursions with Horatio. He was an easy companion; his leaping, sniffing doggy life was a relief from her mother's immobility, gloomy and loquacious. She liked the way he led her with his nose down and his ears pricked and alert, the way his route was never straight but zigzagged by nimble, sudden choices of direction. He was alert to other creatures and driven by inner forces that knew the world in minute and purposeful ways. Every now and then he chased a lizard, leaving her behind, or took off, racing, towards some invisible attraction; but he always returned and he always led her home.

Without Mary there was less of the world to divine. Perdita dawdled and traipsed as Horatio skipped and rushed; she was walking out her grief for her lost friend and feeling sorry for herself. She wanted above all to kill a snake, not one in the house, which was easy and visible, but to find one here, to drag it from its hiding place, break its back with a flick and crush its head against a rock, just as Mary had done. Though she searched, she found nothing. She was just a stuttering girl in a faded cotton frock, a girl with plaits and with too much time on her hands. She noticed that the world, not just her knowledge, was turning to stone. There was a mica sky and a marble hardness to things; mammal becoming mineral, a weight pressing down. The world was transforming.

There are forms of loneliness children endure that adults have no inkling of: stern seclusions, lives of quiet desperation. Now that her childhood was a spoiled thing, compounded by an inefficient tongue and garbled speech, Perdita entered the dreary territory of the truly alone. She found one of the old boabs that had a hollow bottle belly and squeezed herself inside, pleased to be enclosed, imagining for a moment that she might stay there, never to be found, never-ever, never-ever. She would become as skinny as Christ and simply fade away, a relic of herself, stretched and holy. In the tree belly there was a stench of wood-rot and old animal droppings; it was not the fading haven she had imagined. In such darkness she would be obliged to confront her own thoughts, to remember and to feel again all that had happened. Perdita squeezed out of the trunk, maturely extracting herself from the fantasies of self-annihilation that even young children may entertain. Horatio bounded towards her with excitement, his sticky mouth wide open, his thin tail waving, as if she had just performed a trick or invented a new game. She clasped him with both hands and pressed her face against his fur.

As she approached her home, returning one afternoon from her exhausting wandering, Perdita heard Stella's voice engaged in recitation. In town she had overheard "crazy Mrs. Keene" and immediately knew that this was so; someone outside was required to name it and the name had been casually flung as they left the bakers, not to hurt but simply to identify: "That's crazy Mrs. Keene, the one whose hubby got it in the neck, you know, out bush." It was like a brain-wave sparking—yes, it was true. Even isolated as she was, with few acquaintances, Perdita knew that other mothers did not behave like this, seething with words from four centuries ago.

> Devouring Time, blunt thou the lion's paws,
> And make the earth devour her own sweet brood;
> Pluck the keen teeth from the fierce tiger's jaws,
> And burn the long-lived phoenix in her blood . . .

Perdita had not heard this one before—a sonnet, apparently—but knew that Stella's madness had method in it. She almost pitied her expertise with such descriptive resources. Stella was doomed, she realised, to emotional aggrandisement and the lunatic exaggeration of the otherwise everyday. Her redescription of life in Shakespearean terms meant that she was always strung in a poignant register; she was always unbearably, ponderously, *poetic*. When Perdita opened the screen door, she saw her mother staring at the bamboo cage, purchased in town less than two weeks ago, which she had removed from its hanging hook and placed on the table. In the cage was a tiger snake, nestled in a coil. It had within its long yellowish body two quivering lumps—the twin finches digesting—and these prevented it moving back between the bars through which it had come. Stella looked up and fell silent as Perdita entered the shack. Her eyes were swollen and red from crying. She might have been a child, with this posture of brooding disappointment over the loss of pets.

"Can you do something about this?" she asked in a low voice.

Perdita had just turned eleven, but felt she was being addressed as an adult. She paused, considering. Then she went to her father's meagre toolbox and fetched a hammer. When she slid open the door to the cage the snake cautiously poked its head out, and she crushed it, then and there, on the kitchen table, with not one, but three, heavily pounding blows. The thin skull was flattened, the inner exposed.

"Christ," said Stella. She grimaced at the mess and leaned closer as if to check that the snake was really dead. "Well done . . ."

It was not a hunt, or the congratulations of a whole community who would roast the snake over the coals of a slow-burning fire; it was not Mary, seeing how brave and grown-up she had become; but it was her mother, moved by odd circumstance to offer two spontaneous words of praise. Perdita felt an unaccustomed pride. If she had been sure of her voice she would have said something in response, but deciding it was best not to disturb the moment with a possible stutter, she simply smiled at her mother and removed the battered snake, its head no more now than wet bloody mush. She flung it wastefully into the bush, for the ants and crows, whipping it upwards through the sky as a tennis player might serve.

*

Two months after the attack on Pearl Harbor, Stella decided, along with other families, that they would move down south, to Perth. Broome was emptying out; Japanese families were being relocated for internment; even Sis and her children, Perdita discovered, had been arrested and sent away, as if being the family of a Japanese pearl diver somehow threatened national security. Fear includes these churlish and punitive measures. It creates internal enemies, monstrous figures in newspapers. Aboriginal families were sent to outstations and missions; the north-west was depopulated in anticipation of an invasion. Word was that the Government was prepared to lose the north to the Japanese, in order properly to defend the south.

It was a period of interregnum, rumour, alarmist speculation and downright lies. Stella became agitated, speaking almost daily of the "Nips" or the "Japs" and their gruesome natures. She no longer attended to her map of Europe, but became increasingly preoccupied with the arrows in the newspaper that showed the projected route of the Japanese as they spread their Rising Suns across the northern half of Australia.

A letter from Margaret arrived—belatedly—to tell of her family's deaths long, long ago in December 1940. Stella stood holding the letter with shaking hands, remembering not her father and mother, not her sister Iris, but old Mrs. Whiticombe, her hands like sticks, her voice expiring, her skull pushing through transparent skin as her soul stretched to leave. She sighed, crumpled the letter, and flung it aside.

When Perdita retrieved it later on, smoothing open the paper to find Margaret's words, she realised only in a formless way that she had lost her grandparents and an aunt. That her mother was orphaned.

She should have understood by then the signs of her mother's decline: a kind of dithering incomprehension, neglect of her own cleanliness, paranoia, slowed movement. But turmoil was general; there was packing to do, arrangements to be made. Mrs. Trevor, seeing, perhaps, Stella's precarious condition, enlisted her station staff to assist them; and she and Billy would travel with them first to Broome, then on the state ship assigned to evacuees. The whole world was moving; why not they? In the heaving of populations, in the confiscation of homes, this relocation of two families was a minor thing.

When Singapore fell, in February 1942, the proposed shift gained a sudden sense of urgency. Mr. Trevor, who was either oblivious to Stella's vulnerability or wanted with crude malice simply to shock, regaled her with tales of horrible tortures, beheadings in the street and the rape of English women. He would not be travelling with them; he had chosen to stay and Defend the Nation—another man, Perdita realised later, who did not or could not enlist, but wanted nevertheless to prove his own life worthwhile.

Stella listened transfixed to Mr. Trevor's stories. There had been such torpor in the month since Nicholas's death and Mary's departure; now, all of a sudden, there was busyness and organisation and the world war impinging. Ragged warnings flew everywhere, tearing the sky. Disturbance registered on the skin, and in the tone of rackety voices.

Perdita was thrilled by the prospect of a move to the city; she would visit Mary, ride on a bus and finally, like other girls her age, go to school. Yet she imagined her destination with almost farcical error. Since her vision was derived from a collage of images, mostly nineteenth-century etchings, in her parents' books, she believed The City to be stony, monumental and grand, a place of avenues, statues and spouting fountains, a place dignified, wealthy, bathed in leaden light. But when at last she saw Perth she burst into tears: it was such a disappointment. There were trams in the streets and some imposing hotels, but overall it was boring and unmonumental.

For now, however, there was this new upheaval. Billy was enjoined to help with the packing of books and he proved a willing worker and even-tempered company. It was clear to Perdita that he enjoyed piling the books, binding same-sized volumes with lengths of string, arranging them geometrically in old tea-chests lined with tea-scented tinfoil. Perdita saw the world that she had known all her life disassemble; the book stacks gradually diminished, the furniture, spare as it was, disappeared in one day, the kitchen items, the worn linen, these were all packed away quickly. This was not a home that had ever been decorated or cared for. Utility had governed its furnishings and now made for a swift disposal. When it came to clothes, Stella insisted they should take with them only what fitted into two old suitcases—leather with straps, one of them monogrammed "NK"—that she and Nicholas had brought with them, in another time, another time now unimaginable, all the way from England.

Perdita saw the initials as an obscure accusation. She could not look at "NK." She could not bear it, somehow. She could not contemplate what was left from what had been a living person.

It was a typically bright overheated day when they departed. No memorable weather, no vista, strangely illuminated, to set down a future recollection that might return with precision the very moment of leaving. The book crates had been sent ahead, and Stella and Perdita had spent the last night at the Trevors', so leave-taking was essentially anticlimactical. Billy and Perdita sat in the tray of Mr. Trevor's truck and braced themselves amongst the luggage for the bone-shaking journey.

Perdita had yet to realise how utterly lost she would feel; how there are no replacements, ever, for the locations of childhood and their avid, intensified, blazing encounters. There are no substitutions. There are no cunning devices that make exile any less definitive. She kneeled on her father's suitcase, rested her elbows on the roof of the cabin and, looking at the future, let the hot wind blow in her hair. Billy too looked forward. He too carried what was submerged and inexpressible; he too would later suffer from compulsive reminiscences. He rested his right arm tenderly around Perdita's shoulder—he was eighteen now and man-sized, but still boyish in his expressions—and she leaned into him, gratefully, aware of his silent care.

*

I have thought about it all my life, this moment of eclipse. It is perhaps because departures are complex, not simple, that we are tempted to cast them reductively, as if they were episodes in a novel, neat and emblematic. There is a relish with which people speak of their childhoods, but also a shrewd suppression of moments of inversion, when what is deducted begins to define the experience. In the deepest folds of memory, the heaviest sediments, paradoxically, are those produced by loss. The convolutions of what we are include unrecognised wanderings, pilgrimages, perhaps, back to these disappeared spaces, these obscurely, intangibly attractive sites. I wanted a "last glimpse" memory so that I could seal the shack, and the death, and my life with Mary, into an immured and sequestered past. To guard against what? To guard against haunting.

13

For some reason that nobody could explain, there would be four days' delay before the ship arrived from Perth. Although Perdita longed to stay again at the Continental Hotel, Mrs. Trevor arranged that she and Stella be put up at the convent.

"She's not well," Perdita overheard.

They were ushered with their suitcases into a pious room, a narrow, austere chamber with a single bed, a crucifix, and a high square window. One of the sisters, apparently willingly, had vacated her room for the visitors, and a canvas stretcher, still tied in its bundle, was available so that Perdita could sleep alongside her mother. They placed their suitcases on the bed and looked at each other. Stella was glistening with sweat and possibly feverish. Her damp hair stuck to her forehead and she had a fierce manic stare. She gestured intimacy and leaned forward as if offering a confession.

"If the Nips come," she whispered, "we should kill ourselves quickly, rather than be taken."

Perdita recoiled, stunned at what she had just heard. Her mother was ill indeed; she was infected with macabre imaginings and tragic outcomes, stained with fear by Mr. Trevor's terrible stories. If she had not pitied her mother and known her to be wretched, she might have been afraid of her.

At dinner they were summoned by a bell to the dining room. It had been a community of eight, but only five remained, yet to be evacuated. The nuns filed in silently, their heads slightly

bowed, and Perdita heard the rustle of their grey starched garments as they moved before her. Some women, she decided, emit
sound as they move; she will always remember this scrape in the
air, the slight compression like a sigh as they spread their skirts
when they sat, and their chatter once given permission to speak.
Perdita took the hand of her enfeebled and fearful mother and
led her towards two chairs at a massive table. A young nun with
the face of a child gestured to Perdita to sit next to her. When
she sat the nun placed her small black hand over Perdita's wrist.

"Mary sends her love," she said, so quietly it might have
been a prohibited disclosure.

Her name was Sister Perpetua. Mary had been writing to
her. Perdita was troubled to discover this unknown connection, particularly since she had never received a letter from
Mary. She looked into the nun's dark eyes and felt pangs of
both jealousy and relief.

"What's happening?" she said clearly, without a stutter.
"What's happening to Mary?"

But before Sister Perpetua could respond, the Mother
Superior, a large woman true to her name, sitting at the head
of the table, commanded a prayer. The nuns were instantly
silent and closed their eyes for grace. Perdita kept her eyes
open and saw that Stella did likewise; she was smiling with an
air of heretical childishness. Still, however, she looked pinched
and afraid. On the tables were small bowls of a flower Perdita
could not identify—something vividly fuchsia pink against the
white cotton tablecloth. It had not occurred to her that there
would be flowers in a convent. This detail moved her, the wish
for adornment displaced, the assertion, at some level, of a sensual life. This was also, she reflected, the first time in her life
she had sat at a dinner table with flowers. She was beginning
to discover her deprivations.

When they were able again to speak, Perdita learned that the
young woman beside her had been at the orphanage with Mary.

"We were like sisters," she said.

Perdita felt stricken. Their conversation faltered. And the more Perdita sought information, the more her stutter impeded her. Mary was in some kind of delinquent girls' home, but kept mostly in solitary confinement and allowed no liberty. Her main occupations, the nun said, were reading and writing. This seemed such scant and mean information. All Perdita knew for sure was that there was no star-shaped lamp; there was no compensating fantasy of saintliness and dignity. She missed Mary in ways she could not even begin to define. Her throat constricted; her eyes began to moisten. Before her the pink petals of the nameless flowers seemed faintly to quiver.

The meal was of chops and mashed potatoes, concluded by a small bowl of peaches, tipped in segments from a can. Perdita discovered again the fierceness of appetite she associated with upheaval. She ate quickly and found that she was still hungry when she finished, but felt too shy around these polite, excessively well-behaved women to ask for more. She would probably stutter, anyway. She would probably shame her mother by not being able to complete a sentence. Beside her, Stella slurped at her peaches slowly. Perdita rested her spoon in the centre of her bowl. She looked around her. Everyone was still eating. She stared into her lap, unhappy, and waited for the meal to be over.

When they returned to their room and set up the canvas stretcher, there was no space between the beds to stand or pass, so Stella and Perdita found themselves in a sleeping proximity neither had experienced before. They were side by side, close enough to whisper in the darkness, close enough to comfort each other and to find inside the unbounded night a neutral ground on which they might meet.

"What will become of us?" Stella asked, not expecting an answer.

There was a silence that Perdita waited to be broken by

recitation. She waited for Shakespeare. Let it be over soon, she thought. Her eyelids were heavy; sleep was claiming her; her mother was tedious in her obsessions, when others were trying to sleep, or to think their own thoughts at the end of a long day. But instead of recitation, Stella went on to speak of her sister Margaret. She remembered how, one winter, they blew warmly upon each other's ungloved hands, holding them close to their lips, just as the nuns did, here, in their pointless prayers. She and Margaret were shivering, with chattering teeth and stiff, frozen bodies, yet they stayed outside, in front of the library, and blew and blew, until their shortness of breath and the extremity of the cold made them both succumb to hysterical laughter. Two boys walking past called out and threw snow at them just because, she said, they were jealous, and petty, and also because they had no Shakespeare in their lives. Margaret wore a cherry-red scarf and joked that it perfectly matched her nose. Margaret was the only person in her life, Stella added, ever to have loved her.

In the darkness, lying on the uncomfortable stretcher that creaked each time she moved, Perdita felt urgently obliged to protest. She tried to formulate a sentence that would express what she was now feeling: a fondness so huge that it must have been love. But her mouth held back her words, mangled and destroyed them, so that what emerged was a series of isolated consonants, lurching forward, sprocket-like and uncompleted.

"Go to sleep now," Stella interrupted softly. She sounded almost loving.

Perdita heard the sea wind rise and the distant throb of a plane flying overhead. She heard the footfall of a nun somewhere in the wooden building. And she heard her own shadowy fears begin to stir: that like a figure in a fairytale her speech would be forever cursed; that she would move through the world fundamentally incapacitated, never able to express a single coherent thought.

*

On their second day at the convent Sister Perpetua gave Perdita a book; it was *The Lives of the Saints.* Perdita opened the cover and saw with a tiny flare of joy an inscription trailing beneath the tissue paper in a scrawled clumsy hand: *Annie McCaughie, Shenton Park, Perth, Australia.* It had been "confiscated" when Mary was expelled from the convent after she had learned that her mother had died. The book was just as Mary described it. There were glossy picture plates in old-fashioned hues and rather decorous depictions of saints approaching their holy ends—their eyes cast to heaven, their hands firmly clasped. They wore colourful robes and were uniformly youthful and good-looking.

With the mantic enthusiasm that most child-readers display, Perdita opened the book at random, believing she could discover secrets by the mere focus of her mind. On her first try she was rewarded: she opened at Margaret of Antioch. Pleased not only to have discovered by accident that her English aunt had a saintly precedent, she read that Margaret was a woman famous for imprisonments of various kinds. A virgin of exemplary virtue, as one might expect, she was subject to tortures for her Christian commitment before she was finally beheaded. Of her imprisonments, the most remarkable was within the belly of a dragon. She held in her hand, so the story goes, a small wooden cross, and it so tickled the dragon's insides that he belched her forth. She is thus often depicted subduing a dragon and is the patron saint of childbirth.

This, Perdita decided, was Mary's story. Her suffering was to be imprisoned, but she would also burst forth. In the context of all that had happened, her casual discoveries made sense. Without faith, there was superstition; without spoken words, there were written stories.

Perdita took Mary's book and sat on the floor against a wall, her knees drawn up. Above her was a painting, bordered by cowrie shells, of a friendly giant carrying a baby on his shoulder. Perdita would read the book, and then she would return it to its rightful owner. And the reading, as Mary claimed, would knit them together. There would be a surrender to something as close as a kiss. There would be imperceptible continuities and inspiring revelations.

Possession of the book offered Perdita a lull in her fears. Just as she had rejoiced, that day, to see Sis's wave, here was another occurrence of something *returning*. In the ruin they had all experi-enced together, certain books, certain faces, remained dependable. The white convent walls closed protectively around her. Stella was away somewhere with Mrs. Trevor. The nuns, it seemed, had labours to perform, although Perdita could not guess what these were. She was left alone with Mary's book, once Annie McCaughie's book, *The Lives of the Saints*. A secure, pleasant solitude shaped itself around her. In the sweet warm air drifted lilting voices, occasional noise from outside, a banging door, a parrot-screech, a car passing slowly, crunching on the gravel. Nothing to disturb the composed inwardness of her own world of reading.

*

From another angle, Stella is there in the room. There, when it happened.

In the way the scene returns and returns, unsettled, mutable, fraught with the abstraction of trauma and the shattering of time, she contracts and expands by the book-stacks leaning in the corner. As the heart palpitates. As the mouth stumbles, opening and closing, over the cruel blocks and absences that constitute a stutter.

It is afternoon and the day is unendurably hot. Birds have quietened; the dog is audibly panting; its mangy flanks squeeze in a patch of shade just outside the screen door. So much depends on details that are forensically dim, and the blind-spotted nature of a child's recollection. Tormenting possibilities flow to greet her. The vision that rests in concave spaces, the dubious sequence of events, the corrosions of any and every violent action: these assail Perdita each time her mind draws near. (*What happened?* the policeman had asked. *Just tell us what happened.*)

When Nicholas falls, the knife still lodged in his neck—he is being yanked into awareness of *what has happened*, that he is doomed and will die, ignoble and prostrate—Stella is already, certainly, present in the room. She is standing there, yes, she is calmly reciting *Macbeth*. There is no point crazier than this moment, nothing less plausible. Perdita sees how her mother's hair flies upward as if electrified, how she has a stony gaze and a solid intention. Her voice is loud; she is performing on a private stage.

Infirm of purpose!
Give me the daggers: the sleeping and the dead
Are but as pictures: 'tis the eye of childhood
That fears a painted devil. If he do bleed,
I'll gild the faces of the grooms withal
For it must seem their guilt.

Blithering Shakespeare. Who would believe that a wife recites while her husband bleeds to death, that she converts into fancy, high-falutin speech this senseless moment, this wasteful gash? She counterfeits art because blood-letting is familiar and known. Blood-lusting Shakespeare. Incarnadine words. There is more of it than one would expect. It spurts from the wound in a lively fountain. It is spreading, as death must, sinister and unstoppable. The dog is whining at a high pitch and scratching at the door. The two girls are crying.

Nicholas's face is brick-red, then white, then mottled pale blue. He has no dying words. His vessel is spilt. No mournfulness yet, only shock, and the excruciating questions that are yet to come.

Perdita is tear-blinded and overwhelmed. Suddenly, too, she feels drowsy; her limbs are heavy and cumbrous; she wants to sink somewhere, slowly to release, to sleep, perchance to dream. It is as if a cloud has blown through her eyes and into her head, and she is struggling to see, and to think, and to stay fully awake. She stands upright, holding Mary, or being held, but wants nothing more than to fall into the oblivion of fatigue and forgetting. Perdita looks at her mother and her mother looks back. Stella, now self-conscious, stops her recitation. She halts, then she curtsies.

In this cloudy moment, Perdita sees her mother hold up the wings of her skirt, daintily cross one leg over the other, and bend low, supplicating, before her tiny audience. Behind her a breeze has entered the open window, lifting the corners of faded yellow curtains. A map of Europe, covered with spiders, also ripples and lifts.

14

In the town of Broome, everything had slowed down but the flow of displaced persons. With five hundred Japanese pearl divers and their families interned, things were quiet; the pearling industry was sunk. Luggers were destroyed, or towed south, anticipating invasion. Some of the buildings stood empty, or were looted. But as people flowed from Broome, moving to missions and to camps, boarding southward-heading boats, another population was passing through.

Since Broome was a refuelling depot on the way to somewhere safe, American service personnel from the Philippines, rich businessmen from Asia, stray families like Perdita's, were all in transit. So too were Dutch refugees from Java. Planeloads of them arrived in flying boats each night. Catalinas, Dorniers and Empires rested in Roebuck Bay, half a mile offshore to evade the worst vagaries of the low tides that might leave them stuck listing and useless in the mud.

It was a long trek across the sea-bed to the town, so most of the women, children and elderly stayed on board, waiting for the refuelling so that they could continue their journeys. The men came into the town, strolling around, looking lost, wondering what place they had come to that was at once so full and so empty. At night the sky throbbed with planeloads of anxious people. The drone was of transience, suspension, the wish for safe haven.

Perdita was roused from her sleep to watch them pass over; they were like fat-bellied birds, impossibly cumbrous, descending at an angle to land with a splash on the ocean. Their mighty propellers shone silver in the moonlight. All over the world, no doubt, people were moving—armies in the night, forced transportations, the homeless pushing handcarts, men dragging a child, a mother. Even the nuns at the convent were planning to disperse: three more were leaving in the morning for Beagle Bay Mission, Sister Perpetua among them.

Having watched the boat planes descend, Perdita would return to her bed and lie awake listening to her mother's fretful sleep. It was dark in her part of the world so it must be light in Germany. Perhaps Adolf Hitler was at this moment eating a boiled egg, sitting perched on an iron stool with a silver spoon in one hand and a salt shaker in the other. Perdita realised she knew of no other German, not one, not a single face or name. War was like this, she decided. There were figureheads—aloof, magisterial, remote—who must nevertheless eat and shit and lie down at night-time to sleep, and then there were ordinary people, the collectivised enemy, the Huns, the Dagos and, much closer, the Japs. It was this effacement, surely, that made killing so easy.

Perdita wondered for the first time if she and her mother would be killed in the war. She had seen the small army contingent in town, relaxed soldiers hanging about, sitting on steps, sharing cigarettes, inexpertly playing cards, and not inspiring any confidence at all, and she knew of the Rising Suns extending their dots further and further south; they were now filling New Guinea like paper measles. Stella moaned in her sleep and turned this way and that, moving her head from side to side, slowly turning her limbs, as if she was floundering in a body of deep water. Perdita was beginning to absorb her mother's doomed disposition. There would be subsequent ordeals, of this she was sure. A sound like a sob came from her mother's throat. Perdita pressed her face into the pillow and wondered what she was dreaming.

*

In those few days she spent in the town, which stretched in her memory disproportionately long, the way most children remember an extraordinary visit, or a birthday party, Perdita saw how tenuous was the social world torn by panic. She saw a scuffle between two soldiers outside Streeter and Male's store, a boulder thrown through an open window, the shattering consequence of which made her leap in fright, and an old Chinese man struck casually in the street.

As she wandered past William Dampier's chest—a monument to honour the English pirate who visited the bay in the 1600s—she knew with adult intelligence how historical heroes might shift in and out of focus, what folly might have attended choosing this fellow for commemoration. A dog began following her, a scruffy, limping creature, to whose misery Perdita would normally have been responsive, but she threw stones to make it retreat and felt a small immoral triumph when finally it slunk away. Horatio had to be left behind with Mr. Trevor, and Perdita realised how much she missed her own dog, now that everything was gradually slipping away.

In the evening there was a glorious tangerine light, and in an episode of respite Perdita and Stella sat outside with the two remaining nuns and Mother Superior, sipping fruit cordials. They did not speak of the war, but of the weather and their garden. One of the sisters was particularly proud of her vegetable patch. Then Mother Superior changed the topic and asked Perdita about her faith, and when she replied that she had none, interrogated her mother as to the neglect of her daughter's soul. Stella glanced sidelong at Perdita and they shared a moment of exasperation. Perdita looked up at the sky and saw banks of clouds growing a darker orange-red, lying in streamers, astray, stretching all the way to Japan.

When she attended again to the conversation Stella was

declaring: "My religion is Shakespeare. He answers all the big questions."

The Mother Superior looked scandalised. Her blue eyes enlarged.

"This is not a question of literature," she responded. "It's a question of the immortality of the soul."

"Quite," said Stella, conceding nothing.

But still the Mother Superior persisted. She bent her large body towards Perdita and asked: "How old are you, child?"

"She is eleven," Stella answered.

Perdita knew then that in all the negotiations between them, Stella would always take precedence with speech. She had often before felt puny in her mother's presence—confounded by some of her Shakespearean assertions, oppressed by her rules and incessant admonitions ("don't blink so much," "sit up straight"), driven miserably inward by the din of such a verbally expressive woman; but they had also had the hours and hours of lessons, in which they had discussed the world and everything in it, in which any topic was splendidly complex and open to discussion. Although she had always longed to go to school, Perdita had also loved her mother's idiosyncratic lessons, the degree to which she explained arcane details, her cheerfully protracted explanations, her volcanic spilling-over of peculiar knowledge.

Perdita watched as Stella pulled the small table between them closer, took a pack of cards from her pocket and, without reference to the assembled company, began a game of solitaire. It was her way of finishing the conversation. Perdita watched her mother shuffle, and riffle, and deal to herself; then watched the suits of cards begin to emerge and form pillars of meaningless, ephemeral value. Her hands moved quickly and she did not take her eyes off the cards to glance upwards as the Mother Superior pushed back her chair, mumbled something and left. Then the two young nuns, smiling shyly, also departed. Perdita remained watching her mother complete the integrated circuit of her game. Its neatly interior system was a kind of reassurance.

When it was over Stella said: "There!" and lifted her head to smile at Perdita. Her daughter smiled back. She felt proud of her mother, even as she was aware she had offended their hosts and acted with rude and unreasonable stubbornness.

*

Early in the morning of 3 March 1942, Perdita walked by herself, and secretly, down to the bay. It was her intention to see if she could break into a sorting shed and steal some pearl shell, a piece for her and one for Mary. Since the pearl industry had shut down, she reasoned, no one would miss two pieces of shell. The mother-of-pearl particularly attracted her. It had a beauty she mostly associated with light: the lustre of moon-lit clouds, beam-shot from below, the strange coiny iridescence on the bellies of fish, the glittery traces threaded in the border of her mother's Spanish shawl.

She walked through the sleepy streets, crossed the road down to the beach, and made her way towards the water. If she felt any trepidation at all it was not for her anticipated crime, but the problem of where she might hide the shell on her return, so that her mother wouldn't find it. A single plane flew high overhead, curving through, then around, the perimeters of the town. If Perdita had glanced up she might have seen that it was unfamiliar. The plane that flew overhead at 8 A.M. was a Japanese fighter plane, a Mitsubishi Zero. A little later, at 9.15, nine Zeroes would sweep across the sky, bringing with dreadful upset beams of piercing bullets.

For now it was quiet and the sheds were deserted. Perdita walked around the rusty iron walls of the two largest sheds and saw, to her surprise, that both were accessible. One had a padlock and chain, but the padlock was unclosed; the other simply had a chain caught on a hook. As quietly as she could, Perdita unhooked the chain and entered the building. It smelled like the ocean, briny and piquant. Morning light flooded in through a high, barred window. Most of the pearl shell had been cleared away, but there remained a small pile pushed against a wall. From it Perdita selected the two most impressive pieces. They were coarse and ugly on the outside, but their inner nacre was lovely. One of the shells had a pearl blister: she would keep that one for herself. Perdita held them together, as if they were the sides of one shell. They almost fitted.

She was thinking of Mary, thinking in a speculative, floating way about what she might say when she presented the gift of shell, when she heard the faint sound of another intruder outside the door. Perdita instantly felt guilty and afraid she would be discovered. She did not replace the shells, but crept towards the crack in the iron doorway and, taking care not to rattle the chain, pushed at it gently to see who might be there. It was the scruffy dog, the one she had earlier flung stones at. The dog looked up at her with timorous entreaty, wagging its tail in a slight, interrogative way. Perdita hesitated for a moment, then bent to embrace it. Its fur was greasy, and it stank a little, but she clutched at its scrawny body as if it was Horatio returned.

She could not say how long she stayed on the beach, but she was there when the Japanese planes approached. She heard them first, a mechanical hum, dull and menacing, and then at once saw them lined in formation in the sky above her. There was a moment of unreality when she watched them tiny, suspended, then Perdita heard gunfire as seven of the Zeroes flew directly overhead. They had divided, two heading to the airport, the others circling to destroy the flying boats settled in the bay. There was a sound of dense, strafing fire and distant screaming.

The flying boats were invisible in the distance, but Perdita believed she could hear human voices lifted in the wind, transported by terror. There were explosions and she saw smoke in black clouds rising above the water. Behind her was the sound of men shouting and starting Jeeps and running for their guns, and further away, the boom of planes exploding on the tarmac at the airport.

The attack lasted an hour. Sixteen Dutch refugee planes were sunk in the bay and six military planes were destroyed at the airport. Of the Japanese planes, one was shot down; it flew out into the distance, aflame, then plummeted into the ocean.

History records what Perdita could not see from the shore: that the refugees trapped in the planes were bombarded as they leaped into the water, or burned to death as their planes exploded. That there was undignified scrambling, anguished mayhem, and appalling suffering. Almost one hundred people died. Later a mass grave would be dug for those whose names and faces had been so swiftly obliterated, who were now simply charred or mutilated bodies, simply the Dutch.

When Perdita made it back to the convent, still clasping her pearl shells, her mother wept when she saw she was safe. The scruffy dog had fled when the planes roared overhead; so it was just she and Stella again, clinging to each other, pleased at least to have each other alive, and wondering together what on earth would come next. Perdita had been expecting a scolding, but found instead the unusual gift of her mother's tears. But Stella was blowing her nose and wiping her eyes, and already beginning to turn away.

PART FOUR

LADY MACBETH: Your face, my thane,
Is as a book where men
May read strange matters.
To beguile the time,
Look like the time . . .

Macbeth, I

15

Of my complicated childhood, this event haunts me still: the slaughter, that day, of Dutch refugees. I was far enough away to see it all as a spectacle, and indeed I may not have heard any screams, but simply imagined I did, after the fact, as it were, after hearing the gory details. It was, I suppose, a direct encounter with war, but it was also at a distance, and alienated, and involved the swoop of shiny planes through a cobalt-blue sky, the glittering sea stretching before me, puffs of telltale smoke faraway arising, rather than any real meeting with physical suffering. And I was not simply afraid, but also exhilarated, by the bursts of gunfire and the impressive explosions. The small world of stealing pearl shell and patting a stray dog suddenly opened into public and historical dimensions.

In my vulgar and rather romantic imaginings, I envisioned the shadow of a Zero upon the water, then a flying boat instantly exploding beneath it. I had not seen frantic human beings, in paroxysmal desperation, grasping at each other, flinging themselves into the water, watching the ping of lines of bullets chase them to their deaths. No child of my age, no old woman, drowning. I remember hearing too that some of the wounded had been taken by sharks, attracted by the amount of blood in the water. I had not seen the tearing of flesh, or the human made meat. So I was witness and not witness, and in any case, because of my stuttering, could not tell what I had seen.

I know now that I was selfish and opportunistic. To have my mother embrace me, bawling, as if she really loved me; it was like a reward in the midst of other people's devastation. Until we saw the bodies gathered in, and a few Dutch men wandering on the beach, weeping and distraught, their arms limp at their sides in total defeat, we had not truly understood the proximity and scale of the event.

Two days later we were evacuated from Broome. There was no real relief. There was no sense of secure escape. There was only the unmooring and the lifting anchor and the slow drift from the jetty, the subdued quiet of the passengers, whose number included the surviving Dutch, and the catching of the tide, the huge natural force, that pulled us away across the ocean, leaving Broome far behind, tucked under somehow, subdued in memory.

*

On the journey south Perdita filled exercise books with her untutored, scribbled thoughts. Seasick for most of the week it took to travel down the coast, she was caught in an engulfing, queasy unhappiness, much larger than the discomfort of her own child's body. Her insides churned, her limbs felt heavy. She seemed entirely to have lost her sense of balance. From her dingy bunk she glanced at the tilting jade sea in the porthole and swore she would never again step onto a ship. It was like a delirium. When she rose she staggered; when she lay she felt a compression of time and space and the crowding in of images she had been trying to suppress. Everything was suffused by a sour, metallic smell. The air was stale and smothering. It was a half-way death.

To pass time, to counter this dreadful containment, Perdita wrote. She had no actual plan, or story to tell; she simply needed to settle within words some of what was rising inside her. At some point she was coaxed onto the deck to see dolphins playing alongside the ship and was encouraged to walk its length, to get her "sea legs," someone said. At the stern she saw the frothy wake folding in on itself, curling the ocean into a V-shaped trail. It is this image of the voyage, this severe abstraction, that Perdita most clearly remembered later on. This, and one of the Dutchmen she had seen on the beach in Broome. He was now leaning over the railing, alone, sobbing his heart out.

Stella, on the other hand, was revived by the journey. Although she had been ill, years ago, on her trip with Nicholas to the north, it was as if she now lived in a different body. She liked climbing the steep iron steps to the deck and breathing the sea air, enjoying a sensation from some earliest, dimmest time: the feel of warm sea wind blowing back her hair, the tang of it, and its aura of incredible freedom. She chatted with passengers on the deck, and was invited to participate in protracted games of cards. In the evening, several times, she entertained others with her Shakespearean recitations. They applauded heartily; they thought her exceptionally clever. Stella curtsied to the audience and had never before seemed so happy. For hours on end she forgot she had an ailing, embarrassing daughter, prostrate on a bunk, hidden down below.

For Perdita the journey seemed to last for ever. She did not once see Billy or Mrs. Trevor; they were in some other part of the ship, locked in the melancholy of their own departure, coping with their own sense of times and places falling away. Perhaps Billy was also ill. Perhaps he too lay on a bunk, swollen with their shared history, watching with nauseous fear the horizon on the other side of the porthole, tipping and sliding, reducing everything to a circle.

By the time they arrived in Perth, Perdita was morose, pallid and wholly out of love with the ocean. On the dock, she glimpsed Billy for just a moment. He was looking away, distracted, watching his mother. His hands rested still at his sides. He exemplified the confused, resistant manner of the newly arrived. And then he was gone.

Members of a volunteer charity organisation met them as they disembarked, and Stella handed over their luggage with an air of disconnection. They were driven to rooms that had been rented in an inner-city boarding house. With their two suitcases, and a sense of the contraction of their lives, they waved farewell to their benefactors and, with sinking hopes, entered the sturdy red-brick building that would temporarily be their home.

What would Perdita remember of this? That Stella stood for a long time gazing silently out the window. She had her hands thrust in the pockets of her best linen skirt and was rendered immobile, transfixed not by the view, which was of an ordinary city street, with tramlines and rows of shops and electric lights affixed to poles, but an awareness, perhaps, that she had to make her own life now, that she was responsible for herself and her daughter and whatever destiny they might find. From outside came a clanking, screeching, steely sound, like sheets of metal being torn apart. Perdita rushed to the window to watch the tram rattle past. It was the one City Thing she had seen so far that really excited her.

*

It was no brave new world, but bleached and empty. The people in it were worn down by the scarcities of war-time, and not particularly sympathetic to an English widow and her peculiar daughter. Stella wrote letter after letter to her father-in-law, asking in polite terms for "monetary assistance," but received no response. Perhaps he was dead, she thought. They were abandoned, stranded. After the enjoyment of the voyage and a sense of her own emancipation, Stella began to feel weary and disconsolate. Jobs were hard to come by; their savings were diminishing. Day after day she left, wearing her best clothes and a thin smudge of cerise lipstick, declaring her intention to join the world of labour.

Eventually she found work in a florist's shop. Each day, at 9 A.M., Stella helped unload a mountain of mixed flowers from the back of a van, then sort and re-order them into small neat bunches, which she wrapped in cellophane and tied with ribbon. Other flowers, those more ostentatious or expensive, the tuberoses, the gladioli, the agapanthus, were set aside for unique arrangements. It was easy work. The store owner, Mrs. Brodie, was originally from Manchester, and though she had, in truth, no need of an assistant, she felt compassion for the down-at-heel woman with the anomalously posh accent, who stood before her one Saturday morning, asking, almost pleading, for work of any kind. Her husband, she said, had been killed in the war. They agreed to part-time hours and a modest salary.

For Stella it was a relief to have found something to do. The work was decorous, feminine and even a little artistic. And she was surrounded all day by floral perfumes and the denser, sensual smell of wet leaves and greenery. After the hot dry north, characterised in her memory by ugly boab trees and red parched earth, this was almost English in its enwreathing ambience. Glorious greenery. Fish ferns, baby's-breath, leaves as big as hands. The buckets of roses, the pinks and the peaches, the whites for weddings and the crimsons for romance, she particularly admired. All her life she had wanted to be given a bouquet of roses. With her first wage—and even though it was an extravagance—she bought six roses, of salmon pink, and arranged them proudly in a jam jar in their rented room. In a place of no adornment they were a gorgeous apparition. Stella fussed to set them just right, equidistant, equally inclining. She pushed the jar into the centre of their table.

For Perdita the roses were a revelation. She had never seen such blooms before, nor smelled such sweetness. These were objects that had existed only in fiction. She lifted on tiptoe to bring her face close to the petals. So this, perhaps, was one of the functions of cities, to incarnate what had existed only immaterially, in words. To present the variousness of things, the far-fetched richness, the startling oddity of what came from the fabulous elsewhere. And not just one thing, but many, multiplied, in visions, and touchable, real and absolute.

"By any other name," said Stella, *"would smell as sweet."*

A slight tremor passed over her painted lips. It was a moment of unity. Perdita loved her mother. She looked up at her and in that moment forgave her for everything. Stella reached forward and adjusted the angle of the rose heads, cupping them, lifting them slightly, letting them fall in a circle.

*

At school Perdita suffered. It was the final year of primary school and she knew nothing of playground codes, hierarchies, cliques and games, nothing of the educational necessity of humiliation, punishment and spite. Children who carry too much misfortune are necessarily despised. She was not pretty, she had no father, she could not speak without stuttering. Her clothes were crudely home-made and her origins obscure. She bore, moreover, a preposterous name, which other children chanted as though it were a singular stutter: "P-P-P-ditta!"

Teachers sometimes defended her in a half-hearted way, but it was clear they too thought her an irredeemably unfortunate case.

Perdita also learned that school lessons were nothing like her mother's. Knowledge was, it seemed, more severely partitioned, and there were lists to learn, and right and wrong facts. Stella had taught her nothing of the history of the monarchs of

England, yet this was clearly the backbone of Australian education; similarly she had neglected mathematics and geography, two of the most prestigious disciplines. Shakespeare was not as important as her mother had tediously proclaimed; yet Perdita realised that teachers were nevertheless impressed by her familiarity with his works—the only thing she could tell them when they asked: so what *do* you know? And she discovered, by accident and in an instance of mutual puzzlement, that she could recite complete verses of Shakespeare fluently, without entering the word-fray and deformation of her stutter.

At the end of the school term, when there was a concert for parents, Perdita was chosen to stand on a stage and recite Hamlet's famous soliloquy: "*To be, or not to be.*" Stella sat in the audience, beaming approval. She wore her best grey blouse with a spray of violets pinned to the collar, something kept from long ago, stored for the promise of a celebration. It did not escape Perdita's notice that she was mimicking her mother, that from all that was forfeited, broken, lost or destroyed, she had retained her mother's exacting skill. *Unbroken Shakespeare.* She heard her voice swing upwards, unfastened, like a flying kite, clever as any toy and just as easy. For a while she was buoyed; she was in a dream of fluency. From her open mouth: flight. From her tongue and her throat, vibrating with pleasure, came words that had existed, polished and prized, for hundreds of years. But after the performance Perdita returned to the country of her exile. She was again the pitiable child in ill-fitting clothes, who could not complete a single sentence with ease.

When their crates of books arrived, later than expected, Stella and Perdita sorted through them to decide what could be sold. It was all the property they had, said Stella, so they must choose wisely. Perdita sat on the floor, cross-legged, setting up her piles of yes, no and maybe. Stella's yes, no and maybe were also establishing. They compared the piles and in the end kept more books than they were prepared to sell. Both were comforted. The room felt less empty. Perdita discovered *The Life of Captain Cook* and thought of Mary; she discovered *The Golden Bough*, annotated in the margins, and thought of her father.

"When," she asked her mother, "will we v-v-v-visit M-M-Mary?"

"We'll see," said Stella, non-committally.

That was it. No more talk. No concession or offer.

Perdita resented the secrecy and agency of adults. She resolved to find her own way to visit Mary. In the meantime, she tried to meet her new life with courage. She grew tough at school, fighting the boys with her fists. Once she bloodied a nose and felt, for a guilty instant, a searing surge of gratification. Soldiers must be like this, she reasoned, callous and stern, excited by a small channel of blood and an enemy cowered. She ignored the girls, as they mostly ignored her.

Perdita missed Billy. She missed Mary and Horatio and all that she had known. She remembered Billy rolling in the dirt, scratching Horatio's speckled belly, and the look of both of them there, reclined and happy as they came to rest with their faces exposed to the sun. Mary was nearby, laughing. She filled a tin mug from the water tank and with a wide swing of her arm splashed it over both of them. Horatio leaped up and shook his fur; Billy performed mock fury and a chase and then settled to a fond giggle. It was such a lucid moment, returned, bright and complete. Perdita missed them all. How was it possible, she often wondered, to continue with so much missing?

16

W hen, at the end of the year, their charity term in the rented room expired, Stella and Perdita moved into an old semi-detached house in the inner city, in East Perth. It was a narrow brick building, with a fanlight above the front door and long rectangular side panels of milky rippled glass. Something about the sturdiness of the entrance appealed to both Stella and Perdita. With their donated furniture and boxes of books, they took possession of the house in a spirit of triumph: at last, it seemed, they had a place of their own.

The rent was modest, in part because the house backed onto a railway line, so that at all times of the day and night they heard the restless toing and froing of the trains, a comforting rumble, an appealing clack-clack, a soothing rising and falling of sound as the trains approached, passed, then faded evenly into the distance. With each train the glass windows in the house shivered and rattled, responsively energised, bestowing on the building an almost tremulous quality.

Nearby stood a power station, a concrete works, and a modest bakery, and beyond them an Aboriginal encampment, mostly hidden from view, on the bank of the Swan River. Perdita could see a small group of people sitting around a fire; the shape of the gathering was one that she recognised. If it had not been for her stutter, she would have approached and befriended these people. Perdita believed they would understand her; she would be accepted, even welcomed, as a stranger from the country. She believed she would be invited to sit down at their fire. She would tell them about Mary, about all that had happened.

In the long summer school holidays, Stella continued her work at the florist, and Perdita was often home alone, with the house to herself. She created a garden, went for walks to the river, and with precocious fervour began reading more of the volumes that had been unpacked anew from the boxes. Some of the books bore her father's signature—"Nicholas Keene"— and again, as with "NK," Perdita felt the vague presence of something unthinkable. She read her father's books carefully, mindful of Mary's superstitious opinion that mysterious and unwonted communions occur between readers. There were three novels by Joseph Conrad, which she avidly read, wondering at each turn of the page what her father had thought, and whether, from the reticent no-place of death, he was somehow nevertheless present, penetrating an eerie membrane to visit his daughter, here reading. At the beginning of *Heart of Darkness* she came across a passage:

We felt meditative, and fit for nothing but placid staring. The day was ending in a serenity of still and exquisite brilliance. The water shone pacifically; the sky, without a speck, was a benign immensity of unstained light; the very mist on the Essex marshes was like a gauzy and radiant fabric, hung from the wooded rises inland, and draping the low shores in diaphanous folds. Only the gloom to the west, brooding over the upper reaches, became more sombre every minute, as if angered by the approach of the sun . . .

Although, in truth, she did not understand the novel at all, Perdita loved this paragraph. It gave her such dreamy pleasure that she put the book face down, keeping the page, and allowed herself slowly to absorb the words. This was one of the moments in which, with mild-mannered poise, she wondered if her father was nearby, metaphysically hovering.

She was alert to phantom interventions and spooky symptoms, willed them, waited. She now believed in ghosts, even though she had never seen one. She believed, at least, that there are no cessations, that what is *missing* continues on, persisting, somewhere else. Mary had taught her this, the principle of invisible presence, that one must always reckon on more than one sees.

Perdita Keene was by then just twelve years old. She had an entire philosophy of life, cobbled together, ingeniously, from all she had met, and believed she was like no other girl her age in her degree of eccentricity. That she was so exceptionally isolated was no surprise but, like most of the afflicted, the vexed and the miserable, she had her own resources of resilience and power.

There was a thumbprint visible on page 46 of *Heart of Darkness*, the faintest of whorls, a delicate stamp of identity. It jolted Perdita as a sign that Nicholas had been indisputably *here*.

The more Perdita thought about Mary's proposition, the more difficult it became. Since the first reader is the author, might there be a channel, somehow, between author and reader, an indefinable intimacy, a secret pact? There are always moments, reading a novel, in which one recognises oneself, or comes across a described detail especially and personally redolent; might there be in this covert world, yet another zone of connection?

It hurt Perdita's head to have to think of such matters. When she was a grown-up, yes, she would know for sure. She would understand what reading is. Outside, a train passed by with the usual rattle. Her window responded. There was this world too, of machines and objects and other people, carrying on regardless, with their separate lives. At this moment, in her own bedroom, with Joseph Conrad's *Heart of Darkness* open before her and a lovely perforated light falling through the threadbare curtains, she could not see how these elements would ever fit together. She wondered if this was one of the big questions that Shakespeare had asked: how does the life-in-words fit with all these other lives?

*

By this stage Perdita was almost mute. She spoke as little as possible, simply to avoid publicising the curse of her stutter. She was furled, inward. She thought of herself as an ammonite. When she was with her mother it was taken for granted that Stella would do all the talking. They had never discussed this; it had simply evolved as their social mode. They understood each other, wary and calculating. At school, almost from the beginning, teachers had learned not to ask her questions, and other children, apart from their teasing, began to consider her inconsequential. Perdita realised that the speechless, the accursed, gradually vanish. She noticed with a kind of fear how frequently she was overlooked, how she was becoming dim and disregarded in the estimations of others. Less than a character in a book. Less than a fiction.

After weeks of solitude, of mooching, of reading, of distended days, Perdita resolved at last to seek out Mary. To do so she needed adult advice, but she knew better than to consult her mother or tell her of her plan. One afternoon, decisively, she walked to the encampment by the riverbank. She watched her own feet proceed, left-right, left-right. There was only a small group this time, of four adults and two small children, and as she approached she felt her heart nervously begin to pound and her mouth to fill up with clotted impediments. It was a family, perhaps. They sat together in the navy shade of a Moreton Bay fig tree and had, as she had seen before from a distance, a small fire on the ground and swags of belongings tucked away in the roots of the tree. A billy of tea was brewing over an aromatic fire. Perdita walked directly towards the group and a man with grey hair and a creased face hailed her at once with a friendly wave.

"Eh! Cousin! Eh!"

Perdita relaxed.

"We seen you before," he announced. "Lotsa times, walken by the river. How come you never came up and said hallo?"

The man, Joey his name was, winked at Perdita in an exaggerated fashion. The others all introduced themselves—Em, the wife, Jack and Rose, Joey's son and daughter-in-law. The two sleepy grandchildren were Liz and Mac. Joey was a leech-gatherer for the Royal Perth Hospital. He had a permit, he said, a "gub'ment dog-tag," which gave him permission to camp by the river.

"White city," he said wryly.

Em smiled and passed Perdita a mug of tea.

Other Aboriginal people, too, were excluded from the inner city. Joey's family had no permission, so they came and went.

"Mostly the p'licemen look the other way. But better we stay hidden, y'know?"

Perdita took her time telling them her story. Her audience thoughtfully ignored the stutter, did not finish her sentences, and patiently attended as she told them of her home in the north and her black sister, Mary. She told them that her father attacked Mary, that he had been killed with a knife, that Mary confessed and was taken away, down south. As her story progressed Perdita found it more and more difficult to speak; her mind was clouding over as if it was impossible to reach the details of what had occurred. So her version was spare and increasingly vague.

At its conclusion she blurted out—in a complete, unstuttered sentence—"Where would they be keeping her, do you think?"

Joey thought he knew. "Lotsa blackfellas," he said, "in trouble with the law. And them whitefella p'licemen just love to stick us all in gaol."

He gave Perdita the name of a reformatory for delinquent girls, where a cousin of Rose's had once been held. It was just the information Perdita needed.

Perdita drank her tea and talked with the family for an hour or so. They were Nyoongar people, Joey said; this was their country.

"All roun heres," he gestured widely, waving his arm across the river.

It was her first experience of community in the city. Here, in a thin margin of wasteland between the power station and the river, concealed, sheltering, enclosed coolly by shade, she had at least recovered a sort of voice. She was moved by Joey's instinctive magnanimity, she was reminded that there was more than the pitiless school and the anonymous streets and the sense—how it had assailed her—that everything now was defined by forlorn depletion.

For the first time, too, she truly saw the river. By late afternoon there was a purplish bloom on the water, and for all her disappointments she had to admit that it was remarkable in its beauty. As she listened to the family speak, she watched its slow, unregulated, confluent passing. Clouds flowered on its surface, darkened, then dissolved. There were movements below, small sparky transmissions, and something bountiful, unseen. And when she returned to her home she was newly self-possessed. There was a calm to her demeanour and even a fleeting cheerfulness.

*

Perdita waited for her mother to leave for work, then took the tram to the city and then a bus to the suburbs south of the river. The driver promised he would tell her where to get off, and said she should ask at the shops on the main street for directions thereafter. Perdita was clutching a pearl shell and *The Lives of the Saints* wrapped together in orange tissue paper tied with one of her hair ribbons. She was beside herself with excitement. Outside flowed pink brick houses, drearily uniform; there were ropes of roses and decorative letter boxes. No doubt about it; it was an ugly city.

After fifteen minutes Perdita became anxious that the driver had forgotten her, and that she would end up who knew where, lost in these empty suburbs. She made her way to the front of the jolting bus and tapped the driver on the shoulder.

"Next one, luv," he said, anticipating her question.

She was deposited by the side of the highway. Still unused to cars speeding on concrete roads, Perdita crossed gingerly to the small strip of stores ahead and asked at the first one where "Greensleeves" was. The lady behind the counter didn't know, but told her to ask at the newsagency. There she received precise directions. She thought her stuttering made her sound imbecilic. The newsagent looked at her suspiciously, as if she may have been an inmate, or a little slow. Billy must have felt like this all the time, Perdita reflected.

As she turned the corner—fourth on the left—she saw what she took to be the detention centre called Greensleeves, an imposing red-brick building, austere and institutional. In the front garden worked an old man in ordinary clothes; it did not, Pedita thought hopefully, seem at all like a prison.

The visit was a crushing disappointment. When she was met in the front room she was told that "under-age" visitors needed to be accompanied by an adult; she would not be admitted; and in any case, there were visiting hours. Perdita tried to argue but her stutter entangled her, and so, frustrated, she began to cry. She was so accustomed to suppressing her tears that they surprised and humiliated her. The woman in charge said that she would see that Mary received her gift. With reluctance Perdita handed over the orange parcel. She turned away and slowly began her woeful journey back.

17

Of all the anguishing forms of stutter that torment children (mostly males, as it happens, statistically, at least), mine was one of the rarer. Called psychogenic, it is the consequence of shock, or upset or circumstantial disaster. It is infrequent in its appearance and enigmatic in its cure. Most stuttering is developmental, and fades over time; the eruption of stuttering, as it were, is a stranger thing.

We take it for granted, don't we? The inspiration and expiration that presses the vocal folds, the movement of air from the trachea, the vibration of the voice box, the issuing—unthinking, automatic—of air released into the mouth and fashioned by the tongue and the lips, emerging then as socially efficient speech. When it is botched and muddled, when sentences jar at the beginning or buckle in the middle, a self-consciousness enters language that is in the end unendurable. Looking back, after all these years, I realise that I embraced silence and the silent words of books, rather than perform ineptitude and failure. And it was, I suppose, a perilous acquiescence, because the quieter I became, the more others ignored me, the more I disappeared.

My mother, initially mortified, also acquiesced; it was easier for her to imagine me arrested and deficient. She enjoyed her power. She enjoyed talking for me and finishing the ends of my sentences. She enjoyed the concern she solicited, as a widow encumbered by an apparently dumbstruck daughter. I do not think this was any malevolence on her part; she was simply accustomed to discontent and disillusioned with life. It fitted, somehow, this damaged child. It did not occur to her to seek help, medical or otherwise. She was a resolute fatalist: passive, ill-tempered, constantly complaining, and fuelled by a persistent sense of regret. And when I was cured of my stutter, she expressed no particular surprise. Nor for that matter, any rejoicing.

*

February 1943, when Perdita began high school, coincided with the German surrender at Stalingrad. A battle that had begun in September the previous year, was finally resolved as a defeat for Hitler's army, the first of many and an omen of things to come. It was a brutal year. The Americans bombed Rome. The British bombed Hamburg. The Germans finally destroyed the ghetto in Warsaw. Full-scale gassing began at Auschwitz. In Asia, the Japanese and the Allies were waging war in Burma. Nicholas's map, which had been folded away for most of 1942, reappeared and was pinned in the sitting room, above the fireplace. Stella discovered again the dubious satisfaction of tracking murderous humanity, and the unimaginable extensiveness of war-time suffering. There was wickedness everywhere, and vast, vicious events. It relieved her despondency to glance at the map in the morning, before she painted her lips, pinned her jaunty hat, and went to work for a few hours in her perfumed and floral retreat.

Perdita found herself wondering if the war would go on for ever. When she contemplated the planet she lived on, it was difficult to believe in noble purpose, or even vague goodwill. The walls were tumbling down. Entire countries were blighted. Now that she read the newspaper every day, Perdita saw for herself how the crackpot apparatus of war just kept turning and turning, engineering more mutilations, running amok. She began to have nightmares about the Dutch refugees. Incoherently, and in terror, she woke in the middle of the night, believing she had actually seen the scramble on board the boat planes, and witnessed at close quarters the moment of massacre. It was always the same. There was the throb overhead of descending planes and the rat-tat-tat of deadly bullets. The sky was darkening and the water was black. There were screams and confusion. She was holding a crying child. The child was shot in the face and then disintegrated in her arms.

*

It should have been possible for them to make a life together. In their little house with the fanlight and rippled panels framing the front door, settled now, and more secure than they had been for a long time, they ought to have had peace and the possibility of rest. If the world beyond was chaotic there was this small closed space, and the map that converted anguished history into blunt representations. There was her mother's employment; there was school; there was regularity. The procession of days and nights was ordered and planned.

But Stella's condition was detached from work-a-day securities. The pathos of it, and the tragedy of it, was that she succumbed even when externals appeared comfortable and propitious. Stella by degrees stopped eating and by fractions stopped sleeping. She was hard to stir in the mornings and seemed to have lost interest in her work. Perdita was obliged to phone her employer, Mrs. Brodie, and fabricate excuses: a flu, a migraine, a female indisposition—unmentionable, of course, and an easy fib. When Stella dragged herself from the bed she was not responsive to questions, and could not explain to her daughter the sense of grievance she carried about her, enveloping as an extra layer of skin.

As her plight wrapped them both, Perdita chose to stay

home from school to keep her mother company. She would nurse her, she decided. No one need know of Stella's illness, and it would pass, surely, as it had done before. They would battle this together.

Stella's refusal to eat was the difficult issue. In less than two weeks she had become alarmingly thin; her face was ashen and her movements were slackened and old, and no amount of cajoling or trickery seemed to work. Perdita began to despair: what if her mother starved to death in their little East Perth house? She boiled eggs, peeled them, and sat close to Stella pushing yellow bits and white bits into her mouth with her fingers.

"S-S-Swallow," she would say, "just s-s-swallow."

Stella expelled the egg fragments with her tongue. Perdita found herself wiping her mother's chin with the dishcloth, as one would a small child. She would try again, steering her fingers carefully, willing nourishment, leaning closer than she had ever been to the rumpled face, ridiculous and sad in its infant non-compliance.

"S-S-Swallow."

Stella echoed with unthinking cruelty: "S-S-Swallow."

But still she did not. An alien neutrality had settled on her features. Perdita stared at her mother's face and felt she was almost unrecognisable. Camouflaged like this. Faraway and so quiet.

Perdita was also worried by their financial situation. She had spent almost all the money she had found in Stella's calfskin purse, and now had no idea where other reserves might be kept. Their ration stamps for meat, tea and butter were all used up. Curiously, too, her own appetite increased as her mother's decreased, so that she was often craving snacks and eating, with guilty voraciousness, Stella's smaller but untouched portions of food. Perdita began stealing milk from the front porches of houses in their suburb. It was easy. Just a sprint through the unlit streets, a quick reconnoitre, and she seized a billycan of milk in the pre-dawn dark. Sometimes she beat the milkman entirely, and instead took the coins that lay in trust beside the empty cans. When she heard the ringing clop-clop of the milkman's horse and cart, she hid guiltily, like the low-down thief she had become.

Negligent of her surroundings, Stella one day walked into a door left open at an unaccustomed angle. She let out a succulent hiss and grabbed her forehead. There was a cut there and she touched it and examined the blood on her hand. Her response was one of submissive bewilderment. Perdita sponged her mother's head, dried it, placed sticking plaster over the wound, and thought how very easily and how quickly the human body succumbs to impressions of damage. She suffered for her mother. She touched her wrist, just her wrist, and was overwhelmed by feelings of pity.

One morning there was a knock on the front door, which Perdita chose to ignore. It was insistent, nevertheless, and Stella peevishly ordered her daughter to see who was there. Perdita remembers walking with deliberate slowness, willing the knocking to stop, but there was a figure in smoky-blue shadow, who would not desist, but who knocked again and knocked more, and then called out: "Anyone there?"

It was the florist, Mrs. Brodie. She stood in a tartan frock between the panels of rippled glass, exuding severity and concern in equal measure. She saw first the unfortunate child, whose unusual name she could not remember. Then she saw Stella Keene drift like a wraith up the corridor towards her, dishevelled, denuded, with a cool vacant stare, bearing a bruise above her eye the size and colour of a plum. Mrs. Brodie clapped her hand over her mouth—oh my goodness!—to stopper any sob that might arise there.

*

The care she felt for her mother was not enough, they said. She needed drugs, looking after. She was *feeble-minded*. A woman from the welfare department arranged an ambulance to take Stella to hospital; in the meantime Perdita was housed in an institution that reminded her of Greensleeves. She slept in a room with seven other girls and was distressed that the girl in the bed beside her, who could not yet have been school age, cried in her sleep. But after only two nights Perdita was moved on. Adult decisions had again taken hold and configured her life.

Perdita discovered she had acquired foster parents. The Ramsays, Flora and Ted, were both in their sixties and had their own grown-up children somewhere. They looked at Perdita through apparently matching wire-rimmed spectacles, wishing her well. Ted was a carpenter and Flora looked after flowers for the local church. They were sensitive, considerate people, who said grace before dinner and did not finish her sentences.

On their first night, Flora gave Perdita a little pencil and notebook, so that if she did not feel like talking, she might write down messages. Perdita loved the crisp, stiff covers, the blue-lined pages, stapled in the middle, and the freedom to make her silence into another kind of text. Why had she never used a notebook with Stella? Flora tucked Perdita into bed, then sat on the cover describing the events of her day. A trip to the shops, a bit of gardening, a visit to the next-door neighbour, who was feeling poorly. When it was time for lights out, she brushed Perdita's hair back from her face, bent over her lovingly, and kissed her forehead. It was a transaction of such easy, instinctual virtue that Perdita basked in the sympathy and felt the cool press of Flora's lips remaining, lingering there, as she lay in the dark. She could hear the clink of teacups as Flora made a pot of tea, and the low drone of marital chit-chat, finishing the day. A chair scraped on the floor. A drawer of cutlery was being closed.

She thought of the patterns people enter, which might make domestic life so sheltering and sincere. Then she thought of her orange-wrapped gift, and wondered if Mary, lying alone in the same city, possibly awake and thinking of her, had ever received it. It was so quiet here, at the Ramsays', without the intermissions of railway noise to which she had grown accustomed. And in the quiet her thoughts expanded and travelled through the night; her mother might die, this time, of starvation, no doubt, and she would grow up with the warm-hearted well-intentioned Ramsays, but be nevertheless completely and desperately alone.

Perdita wondered where her mother was and if she was eating and recovering her strength. The memory of the purple bruise disturbed and troubled her. It might remain for ever. It might show the world Stella's clumsiness and dereliction, just as her own mish-mash voice advertised a private havoc.

It was almost a liberation, the Ramsays' understanding, their easy concern. Both Flora and Ted took trouble to make Perdita feel at home. They settled her in their own daughter's room and showed her around. Ted taught Perdita how to make a small wooden box; he showed her how to saw, to nail, to create dove-tailed corners. "Tricky" seemed to be his favourite word. "This bit is tricky," he would say, and shyly smile, and Perdita felt a sense of achievement when she completed a tricky task, when she sanded her box, rubbed it clean and varnished it to a shine.

In the small workshop, out the back, Perdita saw how hands might fashion a useful object, how an old man with nicotine-stained fingers might reveal the beauty of wood and the honour of simple labour. She smelled the fragrance of the wood shavings and saw the care with which, frowning pleasantly, he handled his tools. Ted praised Perdita warmly when she finished her box.

"The lid fits," he said. "That's the trickiest part."

And then he placed a carpenter's square along the edge to confirm the box's right angles.

From Flora Perdita learned the rudiments of cookery. They stood side by side at the kitchen table, their hips almost touching, sifting flour, kneading dough, pressing out floral scone shapes, in a silent companionship. When Flora pulled their creations from the oven, she might have been discovering a new world.

"Well I never!" she declared.

It was almost a new life. Almost liberation.

Less than a month after she joined them, Flora Ramsay announced to Perdita that she was to see a doctor. Perdita felt a rush of blood to her face and tinge of inexplicable shame.

"A speech doctor," Flora explained. "Recommended."

Since she was to miss a whole day of school, Perdita consented, but was still appalled that her spoiled and stupid speech would be examined by a stranger. A complete stranger.

"Just to check, luv," said Flora, without offering any details.

So it was that Perdita, only newly in foster care, arrived at a clinic building attached to the children's hospital. Flora wore gloves and a hat, and seemed nervous as she pushed back the heavy swinging door and led Perdita to the front counter behind which sat a uniformed nurse. There were charts on the walls that exposed the inside workings of mouths and throats; there were cut-away anatomies and lurid interiors. A pink and lilac plastic half-head rested on the counter. It had a single bulbous eye and scary implications. Blue veins and red arteries webbed the face and throat, grotesquely bulging and ugly. Perdita decided that she must be brave. But although the nurse smiled at her as she asked her to spell her name, bravery was not, after all, so easily come by. Once again she could not spell her own name without disclosing her condition. Sensibly, Flora did all the talking. She fumbled with her handbag for a pen and signed some papers.

Here, in a small office behind the clinic in which Perdita felt herself afraid, she met her doctor, Doctor Viktor Oblov. A native of Novosibirsk, in Russia, he had come to Australia on a merchant ship at the end of the First World War, in which he served as a medic. He treated shell shock, he said, and male hysteria. Although he was introducing himself to Flora, Perdita listened intently: he sounded engagingly like a character from a Conrad novel. He had thinning grey hair, unfashionably long, and wore a bow tie of royal blue, tweaked just so at the corners. His shirtsleeves were rolled, as if he was about to engage in physical labour. He was about the same age as Flora, but somehow also more sprightly and alert. Perdita was instantly charmed. When he spoke his voice was soft and low, an excellent thing in a doctor, and his accent was sufficiently pronounced to grant him professional authority.

"Very pleased to meet you," he said, as if he meant it. His office was messy and unmedical, his manner a pleasant surprise.

Doctor Oblov had objects—paperweights—resting on his desk, which he took up from time to time, turned in his slender, possibly manicured, hands, and set down again. One of the objects was a glass dome containing a multi-petalled flower of startling turquoise, the like of which could not possibly exist in nature. There was a second dome containing a tiny sailing ship rising unsteadily on tumultuous waves, and a third, which held a butterfly of iridescent violet. As a child who had rarely been given gifts, who possessed a piece of pearl shell but little else that might be coveted as treasure, Perdita found these objects delightfully attractive.

At their first meeting, there were a few questions, but very little else, and Perdita hardly believed that Doctor Oblov was a doctor at all. He saw her looking at the three glass domes as he played with them, and asked her if she would like to choose one to hold while he asked her some questions. It would make talking easier, he said. Perdita thought this was a childish notion, but agreed in order to humour the old man, and because the invitation to hold one of the paperweights was what she had hoped for. She chose the dome that contained the unnatural flower.

"When you speak to me," said Doctor Oblov, "imagine that your voice is projected beyond you, into the dome, and coming, like magic, out of the centre of the blue flower."

Again Perdita thought this a foolish suggestion—he was treating her as a little girl, she disdainfully reflected—but there was a loveliness to the object that could surely bear this attention. She held the dome, which was cold and perfect, which was, she had to concede, one of the most beautiful things she had ever seen, and responded to the doctor's simple questions, asked in a voice so low she could hardly hear him.

Yes, she had begun to stutter about two years ago, after witnessing her father's death. Yes, it was getting worse, she spoke less and less. Yes, there were occasions when she spoke without a stutter; she could recite whole verses of Shakespeare, which she had learned from her mother.

At this Doctor Oblov leaned back in his chair, knitting his fingers.

"Shakespeare?"

"That's what she said," Flora interjected bluntly.

Perdita looked up at her and smiled, then resumed gazing into the artificial intricacies of the dome.

"Would you mind?" asked the doctor. "Just a verse or two?"

It was entirely straightforward: Perdita recited the Hamlet monologue, which was her easiest piece. She heard her own fluency with a sense of pride. She thought fleetingly of her mother, mad as Prince Hamlet, railing, mutinous, against slings and arrows.

To die, to sleep;
To sleep, perchance to dream. Ay, there's the rub;
For in that sleep of death what dreams may come,
When we have shuffled off this mortal coil,
Must give us pause.

Doctor Oblov looked impressed. Flora beamed and clutched her handbag close like an excited girl on a tram.

"I see," said the doctor.

He stretched out his open palm, indicating that Perdita should return the dome. She placed it carefully in the pit of his hand. It caught the light, and glinted like a jewel.

"One day," he said to her, "When you no longer stutter, you can take it home."

Perdita was thrilled for a moment, but then crushed by scepticism. It was hardly a promise he would be required to keep. But Doctor Oblov smiled at her, and reached to shake her hand, as though he considered her not a child after all, but another adult. She took the doctor's hand earnestly, shook it like a grown-up, and was pleased she had come.

As they left the building Perdita's mouth flew open with the surprise of a sudden gust of wind. Flora's hat took flight. As Perdita scrambled to retrieve it there was this physical comfort: grasping the hat, handing it back, seeing with what comfortable joy it was received.

"Gracious me!" said Flora.

18

The most distorted lives eventually adjust, find equilibrium in the new formations circumstances have offered them. For the first months at the Ramsays', Perdita was almost happy. Although she would not admit it, her mother's presence had been burdensome, almost atmospheric in its pervasiveness, a kind of pre-monsoonal gloom, a clammy humidity, so there was a certain relief in her removal and incarceration. Flora took her every week to visit Stella in the hospital, but the meetings were governed by the patient's impossible egotism. Even in illness, suffering the theft of energy and the collapse of her spirit, Stella was still domineering. She spoke curtly to Perdita.

"Why have you come? What are you doing here?"

When Perdita responded that she didn't know what to say, Stella snapped, "Nothing will come of nothing."

Flora said afterwards to Ted that Stella sounded "smug as a cannibal. As if she'd just gobbled and swallowed her own daughter." (Perdita overheard them, listening in bed, dejected.) Flora sat quietly, exasperated, anxious not to judge, but saw Perdita's misery under the curious tyranny her mother imposed. When she was not aggressive, Stella was entirely vague, ignoring or barely acknowledging Perdita's presence. She would turn her face away, and find the smudged windowpane and dull view beyond of more compelling interest.

"It's because she's ill, luv," said Flora.

I know, Perdita wrote in her notebook, underlined, emphatic.

"Perhaps we should just let her be."

Flora patted Perdita's hand. Two nurses had watched the odd couple try, and try again, with Mrs. Keene.

"Bloody tragedy, that's what it is," one of the nurses said, when she heard the unfortunate daughter stutter.

As they left, Perdita saw Stella reach over and pick up the biscuit tin of old buttons she still doggedly cherished. There was a rattle, and a settling, and yet another closing down.

*

On her second visit to Doctor Oblov, Perdita thought again how very unmedical it seemed. Flora was this time instructed to stay in the waiting room, and the doctor once more greeted Perdita by shaking her hand. He sat her down in a brown leather chair, too capacious for her size, and handed her the flower dome to hold while they spoke.

"I will tell you," said Doctor Oblov, with his surprisingly quiet voice, "about my life. Then you will tell me about yours. I will hold this ship—" he held up the sailing ship dome— "because it helps me to speak. I like the way it rests so easily in my hands, the way it can carry my story to you."

Here Doctor Oblov paused to smile. Perdita thought it was like Mary winking when she was cheating at cards, as if they were sharing an illicit understanding of the game.

"I was born almost sixty-two years ago in a little town outside the city of Novosibirsk in Russia. I was from what you would here call a middle-class family: my father was a lawyer; my mother had a small inheritance; in any case, we were comfortably well off. We had servants: Masha, who cooked and cleaned, and an old helper, Ivan, a retainer, around the house. We didn't think of them as servants. And I had two wonderful sisters, Olga and Ilena, both slightly older than me. I adored my sisters and they adored me. They dressed me up and made me the object of their games, and I was happy to oblige. They read me stories and helped me with my schoolwork. Both had long blonde curls, pretty as pictures. I was the dark one.

"When I was ten, and Olga and Ilena were twelve and fourteen, we all contracted the Spanish flu. Many people in our town became ill, very quickly; it terrified me. Olga and Ilena died, and I was left alone. I wanted to die too, but instead all my hair fell out, so that I was just a little bald boy, grieving, and feeling lost and absurd. My mother bought me a new cap, which I wore day and night. And it was almost a year before my hair started growing back."

Here Doctor Oblov paused. Perdita stared fixedly at the glass flower.

"I decided about then that I would become a doctor when I grew up. Later I studied at medical school in Novosibirsk, and then in Moscow. My studies were drawn out and disrupted—it was a wild time in Russia, a revolutionary time, and I had not been long qualified when the war broke out. I was thirty-two years old in nineteen fourteen. I saw things during the war that made me doubt humanity, but I shall not—forgive me—talk about that here. After the war I moved to Britain and became a British citizen. I loved the English language. I love Shakespeare," he added, with another smile. "So Russian, Mr. Shakespeare."

Here he paused to see Perdita respond to his joke.

"In London I fell in love with a young English woman, a nurse, a reader like me, studious and quiet, and her family decided to emigrate to Australia. So I followed her here, following my love, as it were, in nineteen twenty-two."

Doctor Oblov fell silent and gazed at his lap.

It was old-fashioned touch, all this talk of love. Perdita had never heard anyone talk like this before.

"Do you have a wife?" she asked directly, without the trace of a stutter.

Doctor Oblov hesitated, seeking the right words. "No," he said, "but I have a female companion. I have been happy here," he went on. "I like this country. I work mostly at the children's hospital, and have this clinic, one day a week. Now. What would you like to tell me about yourself?"

Perdita felt herself fill up with a thousand possible stories. She held the dome in her hand, turned it and noticed the convex distortions of the flower shape. Everything depended on the angle of vision.

Perdita told Doctor Oblov—stuttering—of her eccentric parents, of her childhood in isolation, the war pinned to the wall. Then, as she grew bolder, she told him of Mary and Billy, how they linked with her, like the dove-tailing ends of a wooden box. There are other families, she said, not just the one you are born with.

Finally she began to narrate her father's death, but as she drew near the topic she realised, with the force of a revelation, that she was not at all sure who had killed him. Mary was there, and her mother, and Billy, and herself. Four of them. Just four of them. A strange elliptical quality entered her telling, a manifest inaccuracy. Her mouth became muddled; she could not speak.

It frightened her to realise that she did not know what had happened. That she had not thought of it until now, nor realised her unknowing. It felt like the upheaval of seasickness, experienced in a dank, groping darkness, with the floor sliding away and surfaces dangerously angled. The smell of something underneath. The sense of up-down, up-down, as waves moved above something drowned.

There was a crime here somewhere, and she thought her mother might be responsible. Perdita had been able to talk to Dr. Oblov as she had to no one else—to disclose her secret confounding, her love for Mary and Billy—yet there was something unbearable and abstruse in all her disclosures. There was a dissolving of memory as she approached its substance; there was a gap and shapelessness to her own lost history.

"That's enough for today," said Doctor Oblov, sensing Perdita's distress. "We will talk again. And perhaps, if you will be so kind, you might give me another recitation."

Perdita was flustered and at a loss. She saw Doctor Oblov's hand stretch out for the dome. She placed it in the centre of his palm, and felt, for no reason she understood, that she wanted to lay her head softly on the side of the brown leather armchair, and weep, and weep.

When they were outside, Flora said simply: "Well?"

Perdita wrote in her notebook: "*He told me his life, he had two sisters who died. Then he went bald.*"

Flora's eyes widened.

"*He has no wife,*" she added in a scribble, "*but he has a female companion.*"

"Goodness me," said Flora.

But somehow Flora still trusted Dr. Oblov. She had noticed how quietly the foreign doctor spoke, so unAustralian. He must be sensitive, she had concluded, to speak with such effacement.

"*They died of Spanish flu,*" Perdita wrote.

"Oh?"

"*The sisters. The two sisters died of the Spanish flu.*"

Perdita was trying to imagine Doctor Oblov as a small bald boy, keeled over, doubled up, stricken by grief. His eyes were moist and swollen, and his head shiny with absence. Solitude became him. She saw him pull down his new cap and set his face in a courageous mask and walk away from her, long ago, in a distant snowy country. He became smaller and smaller, this bereaved little boy, and then he disappeared. Velvety darkness, dark as death, completely engulfed him. It was, she imagined, a Russian darkness, reaching into wastelands and furtherest distances. It was Shakespearean darkness, full of tormented figures, lonely, soliloquising, driven to desperate acts and uncommonplace destinies.

*

As if missing a day of school wasn't treat enough, Flora had a second surprise in store for Perdita. After they left the clinic, they walked hand in hand to the centre of town. Perdita saw before her the world of shopping and commerce, of business and transport and hurrying people, that she had almost no first-hand knowledge of at all. It was a kind of luscious elation to stand there in the middle of town, with trams sweeping this way and that, their bellies full of people who stared from glass windows, their antennae slanted, their purpose tracked and secure; to see the luminous displays fronting the department stores, the mannequins, posed, in expensive clothing, the array of objects and signs and felicitous enticements. So much glittered, it seemed; there were so many reflections and repetitions. And although there were sandbags piled high around the public buildings, alarmist signs pointing imperatively to the location of bomb shelters and lengths of paper glued in stripes to the surfaces of plate-glass windows—a weak measure against any bomb-shattering explosions—the war seemed a long way away and difficult to believe in.

Flora led Perdita down one of the arcades and she saw there that the world of manufactured objects settled discretely into categories and compartments. There was a store entirely of jewellery and wristwatches, and another of books; a café was next and then a store of hats, hundreds of hats, of bizarre variety and pointless ornamentation. From the hat shop stepped a woman in a canary-yellow frock; she was wearing dark, arched sunglasses and smiled at Perdita as she passed. The music of her high-heeled shoes rang on the paving stones. There were bluestriped awnings, lime-green electric signs and red-chequered tablecloths. Objects appeared in crystal light, bent over by coiffed women or men in neat black suits.

Perdita felt a country girl's dumb perplexity, but also an enlivening, a secret excitement; the whole paraphernalia of commodities brought with it such artifice, such contrived display. They were "window shopping," Flora declared. Perdita did not yet understand the true authority of money, so she sensed no particular desire or lack. She listened to Flora's oohs and aahhs with a ruminative detachment.

After an hour or so they sat together in the public gardens in front of the courthouse and ate tomato sandwiches that Flora had brought from home. It was a plain meal, and Perdita felt entirely content, until her attention divided and she thought again of Dr. Oblov's story, and of the little bald boy she had vividly imagined. Then she thought of her own ambiguous presence, somewhere, untold, in a scenario of fuzzy and incomplete details. As she bit into mushy bread around the warm tomatoes, Perdita only half listened to Flora's chatter about goods to be bought and possessions to be longed for. It was mystifying to her, this matter of possessions. She had so much to learn. She couldn't wait to be a grown-up.

On the tram ride home, caught in a net of over-stimulated visions and imaginings, Perdita was now the staring face watching the city judder past. Lampposts, shops, flashy cars alongside. The geography of the streets was beginning to reveal itself. A statue at a corner, a memorable landmark. The inadvertent beauty of this or that vista.

And then, utterly unanticipated, Perdita saw Billy Trevor, Billy, her Billy.

He was in brown workers' overalls, standing in front of a petrol station. He turned around and walked with a stride into the gaping door of the garage. Perdita flew from her seat, announcing "I have to m-m-m-meet someone. S-s-see you at home," and endured Flora's questions while the tram slowly moved a block further to its next appointed stop. She promised she would be no longer than half an hour. When they stopped, Perdita bounded down the steps of the tram and ran back along the road to the petrol station.

There he was, Billy, with his head in a car. He was twenty-one years old, an official man, but still with boyish awkwardness and foolish looks. Perdita stood in the wide doorway, puffing, waiting for him to look up. At first he simply peered. It may have been the light behind her, reducing her to dark shape. It may have been the abrasions of time, the way they had made her less herself. But then Billy broke into a huge, crooked-toothed smile and stepped forward to embrace her.

Perdita could smell oil and petrol and the sour odour of automobiles. The greasy world of car engines. The silver shine of hard objects. Billy was tall now, and flecked with car mess, but wholly familiar. From his pocket he pulled a grimy pad and began writing down questions. Perdita was surprised to discover she had never known before that Billy could read and write.

"*How are things?*"

"*Where are you living?*"

"*I need your help*," Perdita wrote on the pad.

"*How?*"

"*To see Mary. I need an adult companion to be allowed to see Mary.*"

Billy nodded. It seemed to Perdita that he instantly understood.

"*When?*"

All the intervening spaces fell away. They had found each other in this big, booming city, two misfits, equally alone, carrying in their heads a tatty cargo of precious shared memories. Beneath all the errors and difficulties a life might bring, there were these links, unmistaken. There were these small affirmations.

*

One rainy Tuesday they both absconded. They knew the visiting hours. On the bus they exchanged notes, like naughty children, to learn details of the time passed since the evacuation. Through a friend of his father's, Billy had been offered a mechanic's apprenticeship. He turned out, he wrote, to be a whiz with machines. "*Whiz*." He underlined it. Perdita wrote back that she hated school. That her stutter was worse. That she was seeing a doctor. "*Oblov*," she wrote on the pad. "*Oblov?*" Billy copied. "*Russian*," Perdita wrote.

When they arrived at Greensleeves the woman in the front room remembered Perdita. Billy Trevor is an adult, she brokenly declared. Another friend of Mary's.

Afterwards she realised what a peculiar pair they must have seemed—a deaf-mute man, gangly and shy, controlling his anxious hands in the pits of his pockets, and an eager stuttering girl, leading the way.

They were seated in a waiting room of conspicuous austerity. There were grey walls, electric lights covered in steel mesh guards, and an absence of decoration. A door opened, and there she was. Mary halted in the doorway. She was almost eighteen, a woman.

Her lips parted in surprise, she touched her own throat, holding something there, a cry or a whisper, and then she recovered herself and said, "Eh, Deeta, long time. Eh, Billy-fella."

She was beautiful, calm. Dark curls framed her face. Her manner seemed to Perdita unexpectedly reserved; detention had enclosed her, perhaps, had forced a rigorous composure.

They were not permitted a hug, or any touching at all. The woman who watched over them saw this triangular pause, the murderous Abo, the half-witted child, the ginger-looking freak, and no doubt silently praised the Lord for her reliable normalcy.

Mary sat on the other side of the table. Billy wore a broad grin and scribbled a note to Mary, but the woman standing behind them leaned over and snatched it up.

"No notes," she said firmly.

What did they exchange? Mary did most of the talking. She was disturbed to discover Perdita's condition: the spirited girl she had known spoke a wrecked, knotty speech, her face screwed up with effort, her rascal manner shattered.

Perdita told her of Joey, down by the river, and of Flora and Ted. She told her of her mother in hospital and the misery of school. Then she remembered and asked Mary if she had received her gift.

"The gift. Thank you. The shell, he's under my pillow. Good to have all them crazy saints back, eh?"

Mary stopped speaking for a moment to see if Perdita wanted to say anything. Then she confronted her.

"So why didn't you answer my letters, Deeta?"

"L-L-Letters?"

"For a whole bloody year I sent you letters, then I gave up hopin."

Perdita felt her eyes fill up with tears. What extra deprivation was this, not to have received any letters? Perdita stuttered that she had never seen a single letter. She had felt squalid, abandoned, damaged in some way, and would have found solace in just a handful of words. She would have *offered* solace. She would—of course—have lovingly responded. Billy was having trouble lip-reading her stuttering disclosures; however, he seemed to understand all Mary said.

The sisters looked at each other. Mary reached over and patted Perdita's hand.

"Never mind," she said. "A mistake somewhere, I reckon."

"No touching," was the command.

Their twenty-minute visit passed too quickly. They learned that when she was not locked away alone, Mary spent time teaching other inmates to read, and writing to charities for donations of books.

"Bring a book next time. And leave your addresses at the office."

She sounded remote, a stranger now. She was already preparing herself for their departure. Perdita had always imagined that, when she at last saw Mary, there would be excessive happiness and tears of joy and that their tarnished past would cease finally to define and determine them. Instead they had spent their short time together struggling to communicate, and all felt keenly the constraint and repression of their surroundings.

Perdita and Billy left disheartened. As they stepped outside the building it began to rain and soon they were both drenched. They made their way back to the bus stop, up the rain-blue suburban streets, in a dripping sad silence. Skeins of white rain chilled and enveloped them. Cars skidded past, sending up sheets of water. Everything was darkening, wintering, becoming night, conveying in the very elements their inexpressible woe.

19.

The therapy that Doctor Oblov developed involved iambic pentameter, the rhythm and stress of the lines that Shakespeare used. He would ask Perdita to read a sonnet—which she did, unstutteringly—then he would give her composed lines of everyday speech, written in the same line length and with the same system of emphasis. Thus Perdita found herself rehearsing lines about asking the price of bananas, apologising for being late to school, remarking, with ordinary and fluent banality, on the state of the weather and the expectation of rain. Dr. Oblov had pages of lines written up for her when she visited. At first it was only Shakespeare whose words emerged unmutilated, but gradually one or two of the doctor's lines worked in the same way, so that with a sing-song and exaggerated Shakespearean manner, Perdita found she could control an entire sentence. She began to fashion her own sentences with lines ten syllables long, and with the accent as it should be, on every second beat.

"Think of words," Doctor Oblov said. "Divine, bizarre, Macbeth. Think of sentences," he added. "Da Dum, da-Dum, da-Dum, da-Dum, da-Dum."

So Perdita began by rehearsing Dr. Oblov's words, as if she were reading more sonorous and ancient lines:

Like as the waves make towards the pebbled shore,
So do our minutes hasten to their end;
Each changing place with that which goes before,
In sequent toil all forwards do contend.

Rhyme, it was wonderful. Rhythm was much harder. When she was not chanting made-up lines—and sometimes snarling in the centre when her stutter returned, so that her progress was uneven and always frustrating—Doctor Oblov asked Perdita more details about her life. In these narratives her speech was bumpy and crude; she could not find an iambic rhythm to make her own life feasible. This, said Doctor Oblov, was where they were aiming: that she should one day tell her own story with simplicity and lucidity.

"Why did you go bald?" Perdita once asked him.

"Ah," he said sadly. "I used to brush my sisters' hair at night, one hundred strokes each for Olga and Ilena. It was a ritual we shared, a sign of our love. When they were gone my body showed in a symbol what was lost."

Here Doctor Oblov waited to gauge Perdita's response.

"We have no control over these symbols when they happen," he said carefully. "Only afterwards, later, can we try to understand or repair them."

Perdita was turning the flower dome in her small white hands. It was a fair spring morning; dove-grey light was streaming in on them from the high office window; there were books lined against the walls, an aspidistra on the windowsill, a tone of quiet disclosure and easy trust, and she realised all at once that she possessed a feeling of hope. She had been hopeless, resigned. She had been closed up like a pearl shell, hidden in the murky deep, washed by the tidal flow of forces she did not understand. Now there was this room in which a man talked of love for his sisters, was unembarrassed and confiding, was sincerely interested in her story, a room in which—she believed it then—she would gradually relearn to speak.

*

On her thirteenth birthday, Perdita was obliged to reveal to Flora Ramsay that she had no school friends at all, not one, no one whom Flora could invite home for tea and lamingtons. Her friends, she said, were Billy and Mary, but neither could join Flora's planned celebration. So it was that they set off to the cinema together, a Saturday matinee, 2 P.M., at the Piccadilly Theatre. Flora wore her going-out summer hat, a dome of dun-coloured straw speared by a glass-topped pin, and Perdita the new birthday frock Flora and Ted had bought her. It was of stiff red cotton, and she thought it fabulous. Four oversized red buttons studded her chest.

Perdita had not yet been to a cinema, and was not at all sure what to expect. They walked into town—to save a fare one way—and Perdita was so hot and bothered by the time they arrived that her sense of occasion was diminished when they entered the foyer. She found herself sweating; her forehead and underarms were damp. But then—oh—what a place this was. It was lush with a cushiony interior she had seen in no other building, which she would later realise was a distinctively cinematic genre of adornment. There was a thick autumn-toned carpet underfoot and all around hung curtains of amber velvet, parted by silken cords to reveal posters of film stars, blazoned behind glass and inhumanly beautiful. Sofas in the same amber stood along the walls; they had tubular arms with tassels, and bulbous feet. In an illuminated booth stood a woman with a startling helmet of blonde hair—"from a bottle," Flora whispered—who dispensed tickets casually from a large pink roll and received patrons' money with an air of bored disdain. She was the most glamorous woman Perdita had ever seen. Her nails were scarlet, matching her cupid's-bow lips; she had black powder on her eyelids and rouge circles on each cheek. Her neckline plunged in a way Flora would at dinner call "tarty." But then, at first encounter, for her first visit to the cinema, this woman was the glossy and dazzling

herald of visions to come. Perdita couldn't stop staring. Flora
had to lead her away.

When they entered the auditorium it was almost completely
dark. Boy ushers in military-style uniforms with small brimless
caps had to shine beams of flashlight to show them to their
seats. Perdita wondered why no one turned on the lights. There
was a pleasant hubbub of muffled voices and a sense of expectation. Flora was restless and declared that she couldn't get
comfortable. Suddenly band music from somewhere played
"God Save the King," and everyone stood up; this was a cere-
mony that filled Perdita with dull solemnity. But then she heard
a low whirring sound behind her and turned to look. A cone of
white light shot with bright swiftness from a square box in the
wall, and then the show began. Heavy curtains parted in mysterious synchronism, and with triumphal, blaring music a
Cinesound newsreel appeared.

Perdita's heart was pounding fast under her new red dress.
She reached across and gave Flora's hand a quick affectionate
squeeze. In gun-metal grey and white, armies marched at an
angle across the screen, fighting planes dived upwards, politi-
cians gesticulated. The announcer's voice carried a tone of
stern exhortation, not unlike Stella's pitched in recitation;
indeed he was almost shouting the news of war-time events.
The war was faster-moving and less melancholy than Perdita
had imagined it. Sound-tracked for victory, the Allied troops
seemed, more than anything, rather chipper and cheery. One
saluted directly to the camera and posed as a hero, another
gave a jubilant wave as he sped away in his Jeep.

Perdita felt dizzy with the flashing speed of the images, the
number of people appearing and disappearing on the screen,
the detonation of a kind of fear that she knew nothing of the
world. The dark cinema swayed and shifted around her so that
she clutched at the hand-rests of her seat.

Then, just as suddenly, the images again changed. A lion

roared in a circle, there was a swelling orchestral score, and "Hitchcock's *Rebecca*," written in curly letters, appeared gigantically strewn across the width of the screen. From somewhere inside the screen a woman's voice began narrating.

Last night I dreamt I went to Manderley again. It seemed to me that I stood by the iron gate leading to the drive, and for a while I could not enter for the way was barred to me . . . Then, like all dreamers, I was possessed of a sudden with supernatural powers and passed like a spirit through the barrier in front of me.

Perdita watched a spectral mist waver and disperse, then experienced mobility, *with supernatural powers*, as she moved with dream slipperiness up a winding road. Manderley was a ruined mansion; its burned-out shape stood in silhouette. The image rested, then was clouded over, and then another image began.

When the lights at last came up Perdita was not sure where she was. She looked around and saw people taking up handbags and standing to leave, and heard Flora say, "Well, then," in a pleasant, self-satisfied tone. She realised her hands had been clasping two of her frock buttons throughout the movie, as if she needed to hold on to a self that was so easily swept away, so easily transported into the lustred world of stories told in light. The noble pallor of the heroine seemed to stay with her; her face and her voice would not entirely fade. Perdita did not want to leave her seat. Flora took her elbow and gave her a slight nudge, and slowly, still in the half-life or double life of watching a movie, she rose up, trance-like, and allowed herself to be led outside, back into the hot summer's day, gold-coloured now, and glarey, and way too solid. She remembered later how the town hall clock chimed just as they stepped onto the street. It announced her birthday, she thought. It announced the new girl she had become after her first visit to the cinema.

*

If she had been able to speak with confidence, Perdita would have described in a headlong verbal rush—to anyone who would listen—the puzzling transubstantiations she had just experienced, the seesawing in and out of her own body and mind, the stunned surrender, in darkness, to an alternative world. But she had accustomed herself to silence and inwardness, so instead wrote a rambling letter to Mary, retelling, rather woodenly, the plot of *Rebecca*. Cinema was, she wrote, both like and unlike reading, but somehow she could not say why, exactly. As in speech, written words seemed to fail her.

What she wrote to Mary was fatuous and glib and she had no resources, it seemed, to tell what she had seen and felt. In a half-understood and nebulous way, she realised that this was another task she would have to relearn; how to reassociate her words and her feelings.

The day after *Rebecca*—it served now as a punctuation—Flora took Perdita to visit her mother. Flora mistakenly thought that Stella would like to see her daughter to mark her birthday, but found not just the usual remoteness but feverish self-enclosure. Florid-nosed with the flu, her eyes teary with sneezing, Stella was so preoccupied with her illness that she couldn't bear a visitor. Nevertheless, they persisted. Flora and Perdita sat in chairs drawn alongside her bed and tried dutifully to make light-hearted conversation. For some reason Stella's hair had been drawn up into a silver hairnet, which Perdita thought, recoiling, resembled a cobweb. Perdita was wearing her new birthday frock and hoped Stella would notice, but inattentiveness, she knew, was a symptom of her condition.

They were about to leave when Perdita decided to recite a sonnet for her mother, the one she had learned, a week ago, for Doctor Oblov. So she began.

Like as the waves make towards the pebbled shore,
So do our minutes hasten to their end;
Each changing place with that which goes before,
In sequent toil all forwards do contend.

Stella turned, inhaled deeply, as if awoken from sleep, and put her index finger to her lips: "Shhh."

Then, in a gesture of remarkable, almost unprecedented, gentleness, she reached out and touched Perdita's cheek with the back of her hand.

"*In sequent toil all forwards do contend,*" she repeated. "Go, now."

Without another word Flora and Perdita rose and left. When she looked back Perdita saw that the bedraggled woman on the bed, her mother, fifty-five years old, crowned by a cobweb and wrecked by life, had slumped into herself and appeared immediately to sleep.

*

The summer of that year seemed to go on for ever.

Stella remained in hospital, somewhat improved. Perdita and Billy had contrived to see Mary several times, each visit taking a book from the family collection. Perdita stole Daphne du Maurier's *Rebecca* from the public library, and after reading it and carefully removing its institutional stamps, had offered it as an extra gift. Mary received it graciously and confessed only later that she found it dull.

There was still a feeling of distance and loss between them, but gradually, too, something was re-establishing; there was some corridor of understanding they cautiously met in. The first time Perdita tried one of her iambic pentameter sentences, Mary had laughed—it was too lah-di-dah and stupidly musical. Nevertheless, the sentence emerged complete, so they laughed together in the end, both aware of the inherent possibility of recovery. Billy saw them laughing and joined in, unsure of its import, but pleased to find again the girls' long-ago smiles. With each visit Perdita felt a little more confident, of her friendship, of her speech, of finding continuity. She loved Mary. That was it. It was all that simple.

School too was becoming slowly more tolerable. Perdita had earned the respect of her teachers, who discovered that she was, after all, unusually intelligent, but simply preferred not to be asked questions and not to speak. Once they stopped badgering her, she fell into excellence. She wrote essays of surprising maturity and stylistic verve; she continued to fail at maths—in which she had no interest—but was otherwise cherished as a gifted student. When the tale of her unfortunate background was known, she was endowed in addition with a kind of narrative claim; teachers told her story to one another; she exemplified misfortune; she made them feel better about themselves.

She was promoted to the "top" class and in this singular treatment became further marked out and separated from her peers. But Perdita, understanding by now the difficulties of school, was resigned to her loneliness. No one wanted to talk to a stuttering girl, and now that she was "brainy" she was even more difficult to accommodate. Her peers called her the M-M-Martian and when she heard this she thought: *yes, that is so, I feel like an alien; I feel as if I am visiting from another planet.*

Twice weekly the whole student population did air-raid practice. A shrill whistle blew, they quickly lined up, and with swift organisation were dispatched to trenches that had been dug along the edges of the playing field. Students in the Junior Red Cross, or those who had scored highly in cloud or plane identification, led the way. For a time Perdita was designated a stretcher-bearer, but she couldn't believe in this phoney, play-acting war, the way the girls clutched each other and whispered of possible atrocities and the boys, having fun, enjoyed their sense of control. Something in the delineation of roles and responses seemed way too improbable. Perdita began to long for a Zero to appear in the sky, so that her class might see for themselves what her nightmares had already shown her.

20

It is curious the way children come to understanding. I had circulated the words of sonnet LX around and around in my head, particularly the opening, the repetition of which I loved:

Like as the waves make towards the pebbled shore,
So do our minutes hasten to their end;
Each changing place with that which goes before,
In sequent toil all forwards do contend.

It had rested in me, ticking over like the relentless minutes it described, providing a bright, fluent space I could play my voice in. Then, all of a sudden, I realised Shakespeare was wrong. There was no forward incessancy, like waves meeting waves, but recursion, fold, things revisiting out of time. The narrator of *Rebecca* returned to Manderley in dreams and memory; my sense too was of the implicating dragnet of the past, the accumulated experiences to which I was somehow compelled to return, the *again* and *again*, one might say, of moments drastically mistaken.

Dreams, nightmares, descriptions written to Mary; these summonings were a form of backwards learning. I recognised my haltings and erasures, my bothersome blanks. I recognised—with a gloomy apprehension—that although my body had moved, parts of my mind were lodged still in an altogether elsewhere, lagging behind, fraught and ill-fitted. Adults like to

imagine that childhood has a wholesome and charming conti-
guity, but children too know, or at least now and then intuit, the
dreadful fractures that craze any thoughtful life.

*

It was the beginning of 1944, the time of the Battle of Monte
Cassino. The routine of school tends to steamroller memory.
Hours of learning smudge into a toneless field, and what is
recalled are rare moments of drama or triumph. Perdita
remembered all her life her history teacher, Mr. Graves, not for
his lessons, which were plodding, strict and sincere, but for the
occasion on which—outrageously—he burst into tears.

He must have been sixty, certainly too old to enlist, but perhaps, like her father, had been in the First War. In any case he
had a somewhat military uprightness, which combined with his
bleary myopic stare to suggest self-contradiction. He had a full
head of grey hair, and his manner with female teachers implied
that he fancied himself as a "ladies' man."

It was a Wednesday morning and Mr. Graves stood before
the class urging them, commanding them, to remember this
time, this time of "the loathsome ruination of war." There was a
Benedictine monastery, he said, high on a hill, eighty miles south
of Rome, over which the Allies and Fascists were fighting. It was
a beautiful building—he had seen it himself on a personal pil-
grimage in 1921—containing both secular and sacred works of
art and intellect from earliest antiquity. The great philosopher
Thomas Aquinas had actually studied there. *Thomas Aquinas*:
he wrote the name on the blackboard. The Allies had bombed
the monastery in January and now, one week after school had
recommenced, they had bombed it once again, this time pul-
verising the 1300-year-old building into merest rubble. It was
gone, he said. Monte Cassino was destroyed.

"Gone," he repeated.

There was a quiet moment, in which the students expected a homily, or a summary, or a date to write down, but Mr. Graves let out a harsh deep sob, and began to weep. This was not a guarded loss of control but a full-bodied collapse. He was loud and distraught. It was as if some force of dissolution had swept right through him. "Monte Cassino," he sobbed. Some of the students nervously giggled. Others exchanged snide comments behind cupped hands. There was no sympathy for a grown man who would cry over a building somewhere; crazy old bugger. Some of the boys almost spat with masculine contempt.

At the very back of the room, Perdita was moved by Mr. Graves' theatrical announcement. She sat motionless, aware of the varied responses around her, perceiving the spread of this tear-stain from which Mr. Graves would never recover his authority. There were, she knew, whole cities that had been destroyed; millions of people had been massacred and lay with their faces on black roads, or in mud, or in gaping pits, gleaming with blood-thickened rain. Survivors stared from the shells of bombed-out buildings, or hid terrified as war vehicles, hot with recent violence, rumbled by, crushing anything in their paths. Here was a man mourning a single monastery. Perhaps this was what war did—destroy scale altogether. In order to feel anything there had to be an attachment of some sort, a personal violation, a memory forfeited. For Perdita this was like the moment when she had glanced up from her playing cards and seen the newspaper photograph of the weary soldier. The error of things seemed so huge; and the gap between different orders of experience so taut and so meaningless.

Mr. Graves had now crumpled into his seat. He put his head on his desk and wrapped his arms over him, as if an air raid were in progress somewhere above. The classroom quietened. Students seemed to know now that some irrevocable point had been reached. No one moved. Then Perdita rose from her back-row seat and slowly, oh so conspicuously, walked to the front of the room. Gently she lifted her teacher, Mr. Graves, under the armpits, took a portion of his weight, and led him away, out of the room, out of the school building, out into the blinking and unforgiving light.

When she wrote to Mary about this incident later on, Perdita felt a new measure of respect for her teacher. It was not his collapse she admired, but his edifying tears. In her small world there was a kind of seizure of feeling: Stella, Mary, herself—none of them now cried. For all the woebegone and sorrowful events that had occurred, indeed for all the enormity of the war and the cataclysms of history, they had practised their own severe forms of containment and reserve. What in the school had been an outrage seemed to Perdita a breaking-through. Mr. Graves had in some way responded with appropriate distress to a war habitually deadened in newsprint, abstracted into maps, rendered light entertainment. The phrase "loathsome ruination" remained and haunted her. It sounded Shakespearean. It had a dimension of passionate declaration she felt she understood.

λ

Perdita spent a lot of time in the bathroom, in front of Flora's mirror. There she watched herself practise iambic pentameter sentences.

When she had told Doctor Oblov that the children at school called her M-M-Martian, he raised an index finger as she spoke, halted her and said, "Mar-*shun*, da-*Dum*, da-*Dum*, da-*Dum*. Make it an iamb. Think of the stress, the rhythm, as if it is a word in a sonnet. Not your word, but existing in a sentence already known. Put the stress on the second syllable."

Perdita thought that perhaps he did not understand how it

felt to be teased. Children were monstrous in their vehemence, their punishing exclusions.

"When I was a bald boy, he added, other children called me 'the egg.' They used to come up from behind, flip off my cap, and rap my skull with their knuckles. I was a weakling, I cried, so they grew more cruel."

Perdita was repeating in her head: "I was a weakling, I cried, so they grew more cruel." She wanted to discuss this with Doctor Oblov. She turned the flower dome in her hands and tried, with an agonising expectation of failure, to formulate a question.

Then instead, on an instinct, she simply said, "Mar-*shun*!" She had successfully converted Martian to a sayable iamb.

"Bravo," said Doctor Oblov. He gave an enormous smile, leaned back in his chair and laced and unlaced his fingers.

Perdita was now looking at herself in the mirror, repeating, "Mar-*shun*." No stutter, no stumbling mountain range of Ms. She looked at herself critically. She would have liked a crimped hairdo and fuller lips. Better still, she would have liked to be the woman in the booth at the cinema, so gorgeously synthetic that she was a figure of awe.

"Mar-*shun*!"

Flora's voice came plaintively from behind the door. "Are you going to be all day in there?"

Perdita looked at herself one last time. Her face floated, pale and extraterrestrial in the shadowy bathroom. A plastic curtain of crudely drawn fish framed her head. All of a sudden she could scarcely breathe. There was contingency here, and painful faintness. She shaped her lips around a rhythmical sentence she did not try to speak. The sentence was: "I am coming, Flora. Just one minute more."

*

On a scorchingly hot day in early March they picked up Stella from the hospital. It had been arranged that she would stay for a while with her daughter at Flora and Ted's, "to settle her," said Flora.

She stood passively in front of an electric fan in the foyer of the hospital building, wearing a pale blue dress Perdita had never seen before. It had a cloth belt that accentuated her terrible thinness and a neat narrow skirt. At her feet sat a touchingly small vinyl bag of personal items. Although accustomed to Stella's absence, Perdita was glad they were to be reunited. She felt a surge of affection—surprised at its tenacity—and stepped forward to embrace her mother. Perdita had grown and perhaps Stella had also shrunk: they were misproportioned, the daughter now slightly taller than the mother. Perdita lay her arm around her mother's shoulder, just as Billy sometimes did for her, as they walked the sombre route between the bus stop and Greensleeves. Ted carried the vinyl bag, Flora fussed as she hurried ahead to open the windows of the car, so that they would not all swelter.

At first Stella remained staunchly silent, not responding to questions, not offering conversation. But gradually she seemed to sense the Ramsays' beneficence; the fuss was for her, their intentions were generous. Perdita watched her mother make a valiant effort to be sociable.

"I'm not good for anything much," she heard Stella declare, "but I can try to get work again, I suppose."

Ted reminded Stella she had a widow's pension. She was pleased and surprised.

"We can help you find somewhere to live," Ted announced, steering the car around a corner. "But only when you're ready. There's plenty of time."

"There's plenty of time," Flora repeated.

In the back seat with her mother, sticky with the fierce heat no open window would alleviate, Perdita was aware of the fulsome goodness of the Ramsays. They acted helpfully because they were disposed naturally to do so; there was no calculation or pause, no hesitation or profit. Outside the car window the impersonal world streamed by, the mysterious energies of all those independent lives, laborious or playful, embedded in complex unhappiness or pleasure, the lives of men like Mr. Graves, undone by a single confiscation of the war, or Mary, incarcerated, experiencing who knew what daily humiliations and plights.

"Is the war still on?" Stella asked. She looked straight ahead. Her face was flushed with the heat. She had not once looked directly at Perdita.

"Yep," said Ted decisively. "Still the bloody war. But it won't be long now. We're gaining the upper hand."

This expression sounded odd to Perdita, but she was relieved to hear that the end of the war was in sight. It was not something she had seriously considered before. She had no sense, really, of future time, of what life might be in a different field of possibilities. Vaguely she imagined the flapping of wings and a kind of swift uplifting, the horizon dipping and sliding in a pinkish grey light, draughty exposures, vistas, space. The future was this imprecise aerial beholding.

"My husband died in the war, you know," Stella announced. "In France."

Perdita stared at the coral-coloured neck of Ted as he drove.

"How dreadful," said Flora. "We are sorry for your loss."

There was a silence in the car, heated and uncomfortable. Did Stella not remember, Perdita wondered, or had she remade her history? Did Flora and Ted know? She felt a sensation of sudden emptiness, as if all they had shared had been scooped away.

"It was a bomb," Stella insisted. "A bomb exploded behind him and blew him apart."

"Oh dear," said Flora weakly.

Perdita looked down at her lap. The thin bowl of her cotton dress quivered with the motion of the car. There was a vacancy, a strain.

"Ted?"

"Yes?"

"I think I'm going to be sick."

Ted caught Perdita's glance in the rear-view mirror and pulled over with a jerk to the side of the road. Perdita climbed from the car and fell to her knees on the verge; she saw the dry blonde grass heave and sink before her, felt her body's tight clench, retched, but nothing came. She closed her eyelids, nauseous, absenting herself. It was Flora's palm, not her mother's, which came to rest on her forehead, silently commiserating.

21

I n early November 1944, Perdita was visiting Dr. Oblov for one of her sessions. She had been seeing the doctor by then for well over a year, and there had been some definite progress with the control of her stutter. It was less pronounced and less insistent; indeed, she could now and then produce complete premeditated sentences, on the principle of an imposed iambic pentameter structure. Perdita examined and re-examined the way silence weighed inside her, what devices she must have employed, what abolitions.

She had secretly believed—she knew it now—that her mother had murdered her father. Stella's Shakespearean rhetoric led Perdita to suppose she had rehearsed hostile Elizabethan intentions, exultant and fearless, and that her recitations had fixed her on a course of dramatic action. Aloof as she was, caught in her own infirmity, Stella's words still carried a sensuous violence. She had performed virtual murders as other women did gossip, and she had been seduced not by the comedies, but by the horror of the tragedies; not by the love sonnets, mellifluous and sweet, but by those that dealt with the morbid erosions of time. Unmaking obsessed her, and the making of nonentity.

It was, Perdita remembered, not a remarkable day. It was a day like any other. Dr. Oblov wore a starched white shirt and a grey pinstripe waistcoat. At his neck, pertly, sat a small black bow tie. He stood up and smiled warmly as Perdita entered the room, making her believe she was one of his favourite patients.

"Dear Perdita," he said, reaching to shake her hand.

She had always enjoyed the ritual of their greeting; it for-malised the occasion, endowed her with maturity, instated an atmosphere of polite exchange. No other adult in the world had ever shaken her hand. Dr. Oblov passed Perdita the turquoise flower dome and took up his sailing ship, rolling it affectionately in his slender hands.

Their meetings often began with a reading from Shakespeare; this "loosened the tongue," Dr. Oblov said; it meant that Perdita began with confidence, knowing that by some bizarre resource of maternal impersonation she returned to the easy-motion ripple of a sentence. As usual, it was Perdita who chose the speech. She opened Doctor Oblov's copy of *Collected Works* at random and chanced upon the tragedy of *Macbeth*. As she was flicking through the tissuey, ivory-coloured pages, her eye caught, as if fated, on something wholly familiar:

Infirm of purpose!
Give me the daggers. The sleeping and the dead
Are but as pictures; 'tis the eye of childhood
That fears a painted devil . . .

Perdita read the words silently and was returned to the moment her mother last chanted them, as her father lay dying. Fearful of what was rising inside her, a dark shape pressing, an ominous swelling, she turned back a page, seized upon another familiar-looking speech, and in order to calm herself began slowly to read aloud:

Is this a dagger which I see before me,
The handle toward my hand? Come, let me clutch thee.
I have thee not, and yet I see thee still.

Perdita paused and looked up at Dr. Oblov. His chin was resting in his hand. He nodded, and she continued.

Art thou not, fatal vision, sensible
To feeling as to sight? Or art thou but
A dagger of the mind, a false creation,
Proceeding from the heat-oppressed brain?
I see thee yet, in form as palpable
As this which now I draw.

Like the iron gate dissolving at the opening to *Rebecca*, some mind-forged impediment to memory fell away. Was it a trespass, or a reclamation? There was a rush of anxiety and a rush of illumination, and Perdita saw before her, as if cinematically arranged, the complete, recovered scene of her father's death.

"What has happened?" asked Doctor Oblov. His voice came like an echo, from a long way away.

*

That day the air had been heavy and incandescent with heat, the sky brittle, gold. Stella and Perdita were returning from a visit to the Trevors'; Perdita was running ahead and Stella was following a little way behind, walking with Billy, who was carrying something for her. From the distance came the sound of a rusty windmill, creaking as it turned on a single gust of wind. Horatio was lying on his side in the shade beneath the tank stand; he cocked his head, banged his tail once, but was too hot and sleepy otherwise to move. As Perdita approached the house everything appeared as normal. But at the door she halted. Behind the screen she heard the sound of Nicholas panting and groaning, and beneath that, a childish, shallow moan.

When she pushed the screen door, as quietly as she could, Perdita saw Nicholas on the floor, pressing brutally into Mary. His trousers were caught about his ankles, above his large boots, and Mary's brown thighs were splayed open before him. Perdita did not then decide to kill her father; there was no deliberation and no resolve. She simply took up the carving knife lying on the table and walked steadily towards him, enclosed by muddle, alarm, perhaps a dull impulse of revenge, seized by the circulation of her own blood pressuring in her head, causing her to act, to act, so that she gripped the knife and was gripped, so that she saw only a target and fixed her intention.

Mary caught her gaze and vigorously shook her head, and Perdita noticed then that her eyes were glistening with fear. She watched Nicholas's back rise and fall in jerking exertion and saw his exposed buttocks rhythmically quiver. There was no revulsion or distaste, just an absorbing nothingness. Perdita held the knife with both hands and plunged it into Nicholas's back. It struck something metallic and did not penetrate far. As he turned his head, she withdrew the knife and, strengthened by panic, plunged it in a second time, into the side of his neck. Nicholas looked at his daughter with an expression of dumb surprise. Then he grimaced and reached falteringly to touch the knife, but fell forwards onto Mary, his right arm flung outward.

It seemed so pure at the time, so basic and decisive. All was detachment and impersonality. But then Billy was somehow present, kneeling and pulling out the knife, and blood began spurting in a pulsing gush. Mary was scrambling to climb out from underneath Nicholas, to cast off the heavy body that was dying upon her, and as she rose—oh God—she was covered in spattered blood. Her blue dress was discoloured with patches of purple.

This was the indelible, awful vision: Mary rubbing her chest, frantic and besmirched, as if she could remove the foul taint of all that had happened. Nearby, Billy was humming and flapping his hands. He had thrown down the knife, which lay gleaming beside the body. Horatio was pawing at the door, banging it with his head and whining.

And then all at once they heard it: Stella reciting *Macbeth*. It was such an emphatic speech of triumph that Perdita was seized with horror. Stella was gloating, it seemed. She was ruthless, cruel. She stood beside the door with an air of grave formality, as if she spoke as an actor from the centre of a stage. Perdita stepped over her father and hugged Mary, holding her tight.

"Don't tell them," Mary said. That was all. "Don't tell them." They held each other and began to weep.

They were a ruined family. There was such a deformity of fellowship in this room charged electrically with death. The air seemed to crackle and fizz. Perdita imagined fatal currents released from her act, small bubbles of treasonous malice swilling in the air. So there was no subsidence into the quiet recognition of one life extinguished, no appalled, decent or moral stillness, but agitation, words, spiritual upset. The dog, the boy, the two girls softly weeping. Stella's loud Shakespearean voice droning on and on. Nicholas gasping his last breaths, reddened with dying and silently pleading. When she looked down Perdita saw her father's upturned eye begin to darken and lose sight.

"What has happened?" asked Doctor Oblov once again.

The clinic office returned, and with it the Russian doctor, thoughtful and solicitous, bending towards Perdita, his black bow tie now slightly askew. Perdita looked at the flower dome resting in her hands. She felt ill with the magnitude of all she had mistaken. The engrossing waste of it all, the wreckage of lives. In unstuttering words she told Doctor Oblov the tale of her discovery.

It was like a biblical miracle to have a voice returned. It was like a movie, or a fairytale, or something one might read of in a trashy novel, or a junk magazine. Perdita heard, to her amazement, her own verbal recovery. The knotted stutter was almost entirely gone, and instead words poured from her mouth, clear and even as water. Something had opened, released.

"Don't be afraid," said Dr. Oblov quietly. "It can happen like this. The voice suddenly righting itself. Strange, I know, but it can happen, believe me. And give yourself time to think about what you have discovered. Give yourself time . . ."

Perdita looked at Doctor Oblov's close-up face. He was sweating, strained. She saw that he had a small shiny blister on the side of his neck.

"I had supposed," he continued carefully, "that it was your mother who committed the crime."

And then Perdita broke down and sobbed. She sobbed uncontrollably for what she believed was her heartless forgetting. She sobbed for her mother's deception and her own self-delusion, and saw how Stella had not disabused her of her mistake, but in some ways supported it. She sobbed too for Mary's extraordinary sacrifice, and for Billy Trevor's mute and lonely witness. Then she sobbed for her father, who died degrading and degraded, gashed on impulse in a thoughtless, arbitrary moment.

Doctor Oblov put his arm around Perdita's shoulder, composing the shape of comfort. At last, a formal feeling came, the nerves ceremonious, the contentment of a stone. Perdita's body ceased its anguished ratchet heaving, and she felt the intensity of her recollection, so fierce, so tough, mitigated by the quiet room in which she found herself, by kind Dr. Oblov, murmuring words of reassurance, by the high radiant window with its persisting plant, by the books on the bookshelves, the small items on the desk. A sense and materiality of things re-established. The honesty of objects. The irreproachable real.

Doctor Oblov rose and extended his hand to take the dome and indicate that their session was over.

"We will talk of this," he said gently. "We will find its meaning. Now you need rest. Now you need to be quiet."

When Perdita left the clinic she was bloodshot and fluent. Flora saw the tear-stained face and general dishevelment, and expressed alarm. There was a peculiar moment between them. Flora reached out with her handkerchief to touch her face. On hearing Perdita speak—with such unexpected facility—Flora could not contain her surprised exuberance.

"Jesus Christ," she said with a gasp. "Jesus bloody Christ." Then she was embarrassed. "Pardon my French," she added.

And on the way home both remembered at the very same moment: Doctor Oblov, dear Oblov, had forgotten his promise. To give Perdita the dome.

22

There was a Japanese soldier, Hiroo Onada, who hid in the jungles of Lubang Island in the Philippines for almost thirty years after the Second World War finished. He refused to believe that the war had ended and he would not surrender. His liberation came in 1974 when he met a Japanese student camping in the jungle, who told him of the new world and began his process of repatriation.

When I heard this story as an adult I felt I understood Hiroo Onada. It was possible that someone might carry a war inside them, and that isolation might go on, and on, and on. It was possible too, since eighty per cent of his battalion of 12,000 men had been killed, that Hiroo Onada was distorted or remade by loss. I imagined he had lived in silence for thirty years. I wanted to write to him, to express international solidarity. Later I heard that he had found modern Japan insufferable, and had relocated, an old man looped and ragged, still houseless and wandering, to the jungles of Brazil.

*

In 1946, the year Perdita left school, Billy was married. Pearl was as rotund and smoothly white as her name suggested, and like Billy she was deaf. They met at a training school where Billy had enrolled to learn the art of sign language. Pearl Underwood was his youthful instructor, only two years older than he, and as soon as he saw her serious, articulate hands, her unwavering stare, the particular gesture with which she arranged the combs in her hair, the triangle of mottled skin beneath her neck, her shape as she walked and bent and stood, in short, all that she individually and uniquely was, he was entirely smitten. And there was something in the speedy disclosures of fingers, in the fluttering specificity of hands making silent words, that Billy found transfixing. He watched the alphabet appear with judicious pointing, understood the dextrous wavings and sweepings and poses, and realised for the first time his own expressive possibilities. Pearl remarked that he tightly compressed his lips as he signed, as if forcing words to re-route from his mouth to his fingers. She joked with him, and treated him like a man.

It was a slow courtship, proceeding by letters, by syllables, and then by cautious physical correspondence. When at last Pearl reached out and touched his hand, Billy blushed so fiercely he imagined his chance was lost, that Pearl would certainly be put off by his unmanly lack of control. But she was moved, and noticed his gentleness and absence of presumption. She straightened his fingers to correct a sign.

Billy wrote that he had never before been so aware of his deficiencies, and never more determined to ignore them. "*You would like her, Deeta, she's warm and funny.*"

Their first outing together—which Perdita had suggested and encouraged when Billy confided his attraction—was to the Piccadilly Theatre. The movie screening was *The Maltese Falcon*, which Perdita had seen with Flora the week before. She imagined them lip-reading and body-reading Sam Spade and Brigid O'Shaughnessy, noting the wry lift of lips and the haughty sneers, seeing sexual desire and criminal intrigue in wordless and subtle motions. She had loved the bug-eyed character of Cairo, slyly pathetic, and the concluding, bizarrely dislocated, Shakespearean line:

DETECTIVE TOM POLHAUS: *"What is this?"*
SAM SPADE: *"The, uh, stuff that dreams are made of."*

Billy wrote that they had both enjoyed the movie and that they had walked home in the moonlight, hand in hand. He had underlined it: *hand in hand*.

When Perdita met Pearl, she instantly adored her. Her years of stutter had made her aware of the exhausting task of asserting a self in the face of silence, yet Pearl had somehow managed to do so, lifelong, with energetic fortitude. Pearl insisted on teaching Perdita sign language—*"it is necessary*," she wrote, *"for the progress of our friendship"*—and Perdita found in her own hands a reckless and pleasurable flaunting. It seemed a form of poetry: there were literal spellings-out, but there were also flourishing elisions and ostentatious metaphors; there were moments of shrug and embrace and whole body engagement, as well as nuanced inflections of the eyebrow or a curling smile. So she had been barely expressive, when her stutter had maimed her and driven her to silence, and now she felt almost mystically extra-expressive. With Billy and Pearl she discovered another dimension of communication. There were meanings that could exist only in sign, connotations for which only the inventive body and a gestural repertoire sufficed. She loved the three of them together, watching each other's faces and hands, as though the body itself was a kind of book. And she loved Billy anew. In signing she learned again what she had intuited as a child. That he was richer inside than many might guess; wiser, more thoughtful, more given to the marvel of things.

*

Billy and Pearl married in June, on a rainy Saturday, at the State Registry Office. Mr. and Mrs. Trevor were there, and with them their phalanx of Trevor sons. Perdita came with Stella. It was an awkward meeting. Mrs. Trevor, who wore a memorably ugly hat of green feathers in the shape of a nest, was clearly taken aback by Stella's aged and haggard appearance, and equally by Perdita's recovered speech. And since Perdita could not explain in a reasonable narrative how she was healed of her stutter, Mrs. Trevor wondered out loud if she had possibly been seeking attention.

"No," Stella intervened. "Perdita was not seeking attention."

There was a chill between them, an open hostility.

"You know nothing," Stella declared. "Nothing at all."

And with that all conversation between them ceased. Perdita had been asked so often about the recovery she could hardly believe it herself. Only Doctor Oblov's reassuring explanation, his belief in the complexity of the resolutions and irresolutions of character, enabled her to claim her own voice with any confidence.

"There is a margin of mystery," he told her, "that every doctor allows."

That would do, for now. *A margin of mystery.* On this wet wedding day, surrounded by more various forms of belief and scepticism, Perdita acted as a translator between Billy and Pearl and the others. Billy was pleased that all his brothers had come; he thanked them; he mentioned the weather; he joked that the beer was coming soon. Pearl apologised for the absence of her mother and sister, who could not afford the train fares from the country, she explained, but hoped one day soon to meet their extended family. She and Billy were both— how did Pearl sign it?—*"full of heart, overflowing, round as the marbled moon,"* to have found each other.

"Delighted," Perdita translated, knowing its falsity.

There is a photograph of the wedding party on the registry office steps. The bride and groom are at the centre, as convention dictates, and they have a clarity and joy no one else possesses. Both are smiling broadly. They are holding hands. The sign they make is a definite, irrefutable thing. Mr. and Mrs. Trevor are distracted by something to the right beyond the photographic frame, and the Trevor sons, four more, all remarkably uniform in appearance, are standing in a row behind them, wishing they weren't there.

In this, the only image Perdita has of Stella and herself together, they are both in shadow. Stella is faint and blotted, her features bluish and inky. Perdita is beside her, leaning close, as directed by the photographer, and it will pain her later to note how little resemblance exists between them, how even in this most conventional act of documentation, they are still set apart, they are still strangers.

*

Knowing that she was a minor and that with the lapse of time she would not be charged or convicted, Doctor Oblov agreed to help Perdita claim her guilt, and to seek release for Mary. He agreed to intercede and talk to Stella. They all sat at the kitchen table, a pot of tea and a plate of frosted biscuits between them. Dr. Oblov spoke, as usual, in a low, tender tone, explaining what might be done, what petitions might be made, how he would testify to the suppressions and delays that corrode knowledge of difficult events.

But Stella was unmoving, and would not offer corroboration. She stared into the well of her teacup, morose and tense.

Confronted by her daughter's open admission, Stella announced simply: "What's done cannot be undone."

Her passivity shocked Perdita and left her in despair. It was Stella's testimony, not her own, that was needed to free Mary. And she would not be persuaded.

She banged down her teacup, staining the tablecloth, and repeated the line: "What's done cannot be undone."

It was like a door slammed shut. Her face was closed, mean. Stella was refusing to speak when a few words might release Mary from prison. Dr. Oblov and Perdita argued and pleaded, until at length Stella rose slowly and left the room, pitiless in her manner and offering no explanation, tough as a mad monarch, awesomely stubborn.

Dr. Oblov stood and shook hands rather formally with Perdita.

"Write to me," he said. "Keep in touch."

They paused in silence, each knowing the gravity of what existed between them.

Perdita remembered an orrery she had seen at school and the moment she had realised that nothing, no metal armature, held up the planets. They spun by mystery alone; they held formation by a strenuous lace of force-fields and attractions. Now it seemed that something was flying outwards. Something was centrifuged, disappearing, flung godforsaken beyond horizons. Nothing was large enough to meet her comparison. Nor powerful enough to send it away.

She watched Dr. Oblov unlatch the front gate and turn to the left. He held himself erect and walked with a sprightly youthfulness. His body was well-equipped for life, she reflected. And all that he knew was in a healing service.

*

Soon after the strange accession to memory and speech, Perdita had gone with Billy to Greensleeves. She was apprehensive; she was beginning to understand the true dimensions to things. Mary was delighted at Perdita's recovered voice and sat back in her chair and gave a little clap. But then Perdita told her story and Mary listened, more seriously now, taking it all in. She seemed unsurprised.

"Proper good one, that story, like blackfella story."

Perdita looked at her with an avid, questioning stare.

"Yes," Mary conceded. "That's how it was."

She clasped her hands in a vaguely prayerful gesture. Perdita waited, watching her, but Mary said nothing further.

"So why did you protect me, Mary?"

Mary closed her eyes, sighed, and took her time. The release of words Perdita had imagined as an excited rush was instead painstaking and tethered to weighty implications.

"Maybe I was foolish, eh? Back in those days I wanted to be a saint. Or like Annie McCaughie, pure and well loved. But I also knew that I was much stronger than you, Deeta. And Stella, too. I was stronger than Stella. She wouldn't have survived if you'd been sent away to a home."

"I don't believe it," Perdita replied. "She was fierce, tough."

"She needed you."

"No, we've never been close."

"It's true." Mary persisted. "Mothers and daughters, they need each other."

Here she halted, waited. Billy was staring into his lap, unsure of his role. The room was stuffy and overheated, and all felt its smothering claim on them.

"Anyway," Mary added, "too much time has passed. I'm useful here. I teach reading and writing. I have my friends, my place."

There was a calmness to her tone that Perdita found disturbing. From an adjacent room came a clanging, a noisy irritation.

"Mary?"

"Deeta, I chose. I chose to help you, eh? And now I have no choice. No one will believe the word of a bush blackfella. Unless," she added, "they're confessing a crime."

Mary paused. She looked away. The clanging sound—something metallic being loaded and shifted—ceased to meet her silence.

"I understood this long time." It was her old, Aboriginal voice. "That Stella, that one Stella, she would never help me."

"I can," Perdita insisted. "I can write letters, visit lawyers. I can tell them the truth."

"They won't want to know."

"But it was me . . ."

"Yeah, Deeta, it was you. And you were a child. *A child*, Deeta."

"I knew what I was doing."

Such simple words. And such insufficiency.

"You were a child. How could you know? You were only trying to help me. Sisters, eh?"

Perdita looked down, ashamed in the face of Mary's generosity. She carried the burden of such vast wrongdoing. There was no honour here, to know Mary was blameless and imprisoned by something unspoken.

"Still sisters?" Perdita asked.

"Yeah," said Mary. "Course we are, bloody oath."

But although it was offered, there was no atonement. There was no reparation.

That was the point, Perdita would realise much later, at which, in humility, she should have said "sorry." She should have imagined what kind of imprisonment this was, to be closed against the rustle of leaves and the feel of wind and of rain, to be taken from her place, her own place, where her mother had died, to be sealed in the forgetfulness of someone else's crime. Perdita should have been otherwise. She should have said "sorry."

The clanging started again. Mary changed the subject.

Now, so much later, she was still sitting in the same chair, still somehow stuck. Time had made rotten her good intentions, had confounded and deformed what she had not had the courage to say.

How long a time lies in one little word?

Billy was sitting beside her, as he always did, leaning to the left. He was gesturing happily. Perdita had just told Mary of Billy's love.

"I need to meet Pearl," Mary said to Billy, mouthing her words carefully.

"She'd love to meet you," Billy signed, and Perdita translated.

"For the sign language," Mary explained. "There is a deaf girl here, a Noongah girl from Mogumber Mission. I could learn sign language and teach her. And then talk to you too."

So it was that they became a new community of four, all repudiating the clumsy instrument of human speech, and participating instead in the silent articulations of the body. Mary learned very quickly, much quicker than Perdita, and had an emphatic, declarative style. Her hands were ample gadgets, her spirit was enlivened. Pearl joked that Mary signed with an Aboriginal accent, and Mary was charmed by this quirky, possibly accurate, description.

They entrusted to each other the conversion of words to embodied tokens; they watched each other attentively, seeing voices; they developed an idiom, an idiolect, and withstood the derision of the Greensleeves staff to communicate with eloquent pleasure.

The secrecy of their meanings was troubling to the institution, but there were no rules, apparently, against speechless meetings. No lopsided knowing, no fraught mistranslation; this was a language rich with hidden density, such as the body itself carries, and soulful as each distinctive, utterly distinctive, signer.

And with Pearl, Mary rediscovered her sense of humour. Perdita watched as small gestures emerged as a laugh; she saw how it was a gift they exchanged, this sculpture of analogies, hints and mime; how much, potentially comic, resided there, how much, bracketed by arms, was yet to be expressed. Mary practised diligently: a "natural," Pearl signed. They met thrice weekly, each looking forward to the fun of it, to the new meanings they might make.

Five months later, on her twentieth birthday, Mary was moved from the juvenile detention centre to a women's prison. Only "blood" relatives, they were told, were permitted to visit. It was another breaking open. Another smashed form. Although Perdita, Billy and Pearl all wrote to Mary, each grieved the loss of their hands full of signs they had been prepared to offer her, and the frail shape of new family they had made together.

*

As an adult, absorbed in a novel, Perdita remembered the companionship she shared with Mary in reading. There was nothing quite like this earnest, indulgent privacy. In a life distracted, noisy, shredded by trivial social encounters and the too-much reality of the banal everyday, to settle quietly with a novel—its continuous thought, its completed world, its parallel universe—will comfort and reassure her. Of what? Of established order, at least. Of pattern and of meaning, even if notional.

Something else. She will remember, long ago, Mary's hands fashioning a cat's cradle from string. It was elaborate and complicated. She held up her design, her fingers wide-spread, and looked pleased with herself. Nets, webs, cords intertwining. There was no beginning or end. It might have been the design of a universe.

"What's it called?" Perdita had asked. "What does it mean?"

"My secret," said Mary. "My secret secret."

She was adamant and stubborn; she would not tell. Perdita learned then that Mary was not her mirror, that she had an autonomy no simple category could contain. And her own secrets, too, crisscrossing, unnamed, extraordinary as the patterns imagined in the stars, complex as the tracks that configured the desert.

*

In the purple of late night-time, Perdita heard her mother chanting:

I wasted time, and now time doth waste me;
For now hath time made me his numbering clock:
My thoughts are minutes, and with sighs they jar
Their watches on unto mine eyes, the outward watch,
Whereto my finger, like a dial's point,
Is pointing still, in cleansing them from tears.
Now, sir, the sounds that tells what hour it is
Are clamorous groans which strike upon my heart . . .

Stella looked up and saw Perdita standing in the doorway.

"King Richard," she said meekly. "He's in prison, and miserable."

"Ah," said Perdita. *In prison, miserable.*

Her mother had fewer times, nowadays, of coherent speech. Dementia was setting in. After such a tormented inner life, vibrant with nasty detail and Elizabethan distress, Stella had begun to wane and blur. After the railway station, with its oppressive crowding and noise, after the encumbering weight of her Shakespearean filter on the world, so wordy and metaphoric, so violent and time-bound, Stella was slipping away, finding her own sanctuary.

By the age of sixty-five she would be entirely wordless and lost. She was grubby and spent hours fidgeting with her buttons and buttonholes. She did not recognise her daughter, or know, any longer, her sins of omission and commission.

The pathos of her life, Perdita thought, was after all unspeakable. No sign could express it. No hand could draw it in the air. Perdita lay awake at night wondering why she had become Echo to Stella's Narcissus, why their lives had been so pitched in the tenor of melodrama. She wondered—she will wonder, in fact, all the days of her life—why it was that she actually *forgot*. And why she must now remember her forgetting.

In the darkness Perdita was vulnerable to the words of Shakespeare. They flowed into her, insinuating, like unbidden memory. She wanted *sleep that knits up the ravelled sleeve of care*. She wanted silence. She feared, above all, becoming her mother. In the darkness, too, Perdita was seeking forgiveness. Lying on her side, looking in private reverie at the charcoal outline of the bed-lamp she had decided not to turn on, absorbed by memories she could neither settle nor dispel, she wondered what she would say to Mary if they were alone together now, lying side by side as they had as children. And what would she say if her father materialised here, like Hamlet's father, to speak of murder and injustice. Could any words utter the contents of so truant a heart?

What returned to her was the image of the V-shaped trail that unrolled in neat turmoil behind a travelling ship, the ocean marked impermanently by the passage from one life to another, the sign of an everlasting, absorbing divergence. From the ship's railing, looking down, it had been a beautiful thing. Folding water. Turning light. The dreamy curl of any journey. Now Perdita could not erase what returned only as a symbol.

Peace-time at last came, first as a rumour, then as news, then as a public celebration. But after the initial trembling astonishment, even euphoria, there had been a sense of hollowing out, of meaning gone. Like a faded transparency, the look of things changed. There was a stale and weary quality to climbing on a tram, watching the city rumble by, seeing returned soldiers, still in uniform, wandering about with absent looks on their sepia faces.

But nothing ever entirely ceases: Perdita knew this. So the wars moved elsewhere—she would never stop hearing of them—and she languished in her own creaturely, receded state, waiting, it seemed, always somehow waiting.

What life did she find, beyond all this quiet and fury, beyond her idiot, strutting and fretting self? They had no money, Stella and she, so when the time came, and even with a scholarship, Perdita was unable to take a place at university. Instead she gained a position as a trainee librarian. This suited her well. There was a dignity in libraries; it was an honourable job. She admired the atmosphere of muffled restraint and the beige, dusty light. She admired the way book-stacks constructed a mini-city, the labyrinths of silent, orderly words. To see the spines aligned, each with its title, author and organising number, was a particular comfort. When she looked down on the head of a child, bent intently over a book, she wanted to kiss the nape of her neck. When she handed a volume to an old lady she felt, in her very bones, continuities here, the families of readership.

But there was also loneliness and a dwindling faith in what meanings might be found. Furtively, Perdita practised sortilege, opening books at random to seek out sudden understandings. She saw "transmission," "leaf," "tomorrow," "face." Her mind spun on possibilities: *tomorrow and tomorrow and tomorrow*. All these collected words, bound within covers, and here she was, stuck with atomistic, contingent play. Words left their logical clusters and flew apart. Each book she fetched from its slot, sliding it into her hands, made meaning harder.

Perdita struggled in the still space, surrounded by motionless bookcases, bespectacled readers and metal trolleys, against an inner disturbance that had never quite resolved. She was nineteen years old. She roamed among books, went to the cinema with Flora, cared for her mother and wrote to Mary. It felt like an empty life.

One year later Perdita became godmother to Billy and Pearl's twin daughters. Peace-time girls, she thought of them. Neither was deaf, and she was charged with the task of conversation and reading them stories. As they grew she saw how Alison and Catherine fluctuated with ease between the worlds of verbal expression and sign. With their parents they practised a second body, holding up their fingers, enlarging their physical vocabularies; with her they loved sing-song, pun, narrative and rhyme. How their little mouths chattered. She bounced them on her lap, offered kisses, received them. Read stories of fire engines, trolls, princesses, frogs. Slowly, speaking to children, taking care with words, she became their "Aunty Deeta," a slender good-looking woman, almost ready for the world. There was a routine to things that was almost equilibrium: Perdita assembled her new self into a precarious unity, the aunt that she was, the librarian, the attentive, caring daughter. She balanced there, existing. As one does.

What came next to mark her life was unexpected. Perdita opened a letter from the woman who had once been Sister Perpetua. She had left the order and was now working as a nurse in the city. There had been a death in the gaol, Perpetua wrote. Mary had died of appendicitis. *Mary had died.*

There was no suicide and no allegation of foul play. "*A tragic loss . . . in the hands of God.*" She knew of Mary's long correspondence with Perdita, and thought she should be informed of her friend's sad passing. Here returned to you, Perpetua wrote, is the book you shared, Mary's personal copy of *The Lives of the Saints.*

The letter was shockingly straightforward and matter of fact, as though Mary had just been a name, or a casual acquaintance. Perdita felt a crush in her chest and the world collapsing. She felt woozy, ill. Blotted heaven. Cancelled love. *Oh God. Mary*.

It was such a humble parcel, wrapped in brown paper, and tied crosswise with string. Perdita held it for a while, unable to act. The weight of what lay, interleaved, in any lives. Of what existed between girls long ago, in a doom-laden story. In warm, yellow light, Perdita unwrapped the book, folding back the planes of the paper, carefully smoothing them as she went. Her hands were trembling. Slowly she ran her fingertips along the paper creases. She rolled the string into a little ball. She placed her palm gently across the cover and held it there, pausing.

She sat still, staring into space at nothing, and then more nothing. Nothing, more nothing. Light fell on the kitchen table in a neat clear square. When Perdita unwrapped the book, the past came rushing to meet her.

And only then, turning the pages, peering at what Mary had read, did she begin to know, did she begin to open and grieve. There was a flood of hot tears, and a sudden heart breaking.

I should have said sorry to my sister, Mary. Sorry, my sister, oh my sister, sorry.

23

What remains is broken as my speech once was. But I see now what my tongue-tied misery could not: the shape that affections make, the patterns that love upholds in the face of any shattering. It is not sentimentality that drives me to claim this, but the need—more explicitly self-serving, perhaps—to imagine something venerable and illustrious beneath such waste.

It is an image of our house, seen at night from outside, that I continually revisit, as though I have converted my history into the opening shot of a second-rate movie. This was the night Stella and I returned after the murder. Mr. Trevor had gone earlier to light the kerosene lamps, and as we came upon it, beneath a three-quarter moon, I saw emblematically the shape I would seal my secret within. I was already choked by words and inexpressive, I already had a cramped and mangled speech; here was the shape to contain my calamity.

Houses seen from outside, at night, convey a particular beauty. Their windows are bright beacons, their violet outlines, etched indistinctly against the star-dark sky, have a somewhat mythic implication of shelter and repose. Our house was smaller in the darkness, but more mysterious. Moon shadows fell across its doorways and slanted surfaces, there was a gleam on the iron roof—the corrugations appearing as ripples—and a dark square of void towards the back.

I was afraid to re-enter our house, but I think now that the return enabled my distinctive forgetting. As I crossed the threshold of the doorway, pushing back the screen door, I saw a multicoloured patched rug, a disguise, a deletion, and no longer knew exactly what had happened in that room.

Stella was abnormally loud and assertive, while I merged into the inertia of denial and repression. Three lamps, each producing a soft copper flare, triangulated my mother as she moved about the room, touching the map, the newspaper cuttings, the spines of our books, as if she was securing them in their places, or conferring new meaning. I remember my prevarication, my intermediate state. I remember standing still, watching her, wondering what on earth would happen next.

The details remain: Stella had a button missing on her blouse. Her fingers played around the buttonhole and fidgeted at the gape. Horatio was inside, sniffing in corners, restless, looking with doggy incomprehension around him. I called him, held his head, and scratched behind his ears; then Stella ordered that he be put outside for the night. There were moths banging at the windows, brown dusty shapes, and the night cries of swift, predatory birds. There was the stench of cleaning powder and smoke, my mother's mobile shadow, a bulbous teapot on the table, with unfamiliar tin mugs, left behind by Mrs. Trevor when she made tea for the policemen.

What was lost and what remained. What was absorbed into the dateless darkness of my father's death, and what irresistibly persisted, the visible, the present, the shamelessly alive. I knew there were compartments of memory and feeling I had begun to seal; and although I did not will it, I was already selecting what to forget. Events were folding away, finding pleats of the self. The shadows of night were beginning to invade.

Stella darkened all the lamps but one, which she took into her room. Another detail—the acrid smell of kerosene, sharper this night than at any other time in my childhood. Stella did not say good night, she simply retreated, preoccupied. There was the sound of a drawer being opened, of rustling clothes, of shoes dropped to the floor. Rather than stay wide awake, and alone, where violence had happened, I crept outside. Beneath the gleaming night sky I lay on the earth with Horatio. I buried my face in his belly and listened to the rhythm of his sleeping.

Afraid of slumbery agitation, or ghostly visits, I willed myself to think instead of Stella's snow dream: a field of flakes descending, the slow transformation of the shapes of the world, the slow, inconclusive, obliteration. I saw a distant place, all forgetful white, reversing its presences. I saw Mary, and Billy, covered by snowflakes. I saw my mother's bare feet beneath the hem of her nightgown. Everything was losing definition and outline. Everything was disappearing under the gradual snow. Calmed, I looked at the sky and saw only a blank. Soft curtains coming down, a whiteness, a peace.

The word "sorry" has dense and complicated meanings in Australia.

In April 1997 a report by the Human Rights and Equal Opportunity Commission (HREOC) entitled "Bringing them Home: Report of the National Inquiry into the Separation of Aboriginal and Torres Strait Islander Children from their Families" was tabled in the Australian parliament. It is based on 777 submissions (of which 500 were confidential) enquiring into the forcible removal of thousands of Aboriginal and Torres Strait Islander children from their families. It is a moving and distressing document of the emotional and physical suffering of the people who have become known as the "Stolen Generations." The federal policy of "removing" children continued until the early 1970s.

At an Australian Reconciliation Convention held in Melbourne in May 1997, then Prime Minister John Howard refused to say "sorry" to Aboriginal Australians for past government policies of mistreatment. The audience at the convention rose and turned their backs to the prime minister, shaming him in a silent protest with their bodies. Prime Minister Howard has since refused on many occasions to say "sorry."

One of the recommendations of the "Bringing them Home" report was that a National Sorry Day should be declared. On 26 May 1998, one year after the tabling of the report, the first "National Sorry Day" was held. It offered the community the opportunity to be involved in activities to acknowledge the impact of the policies of forcible removal on Aus-tralia's indigenous populations. A huge range of community activities took place across Australia on Sorry Day in 1998, including marches for reconciliation in all major cities. Sorry Books, in which people could record their personal feelings, were presented to representatives of indigenous communities.

Hundreds of thousands of signatures were received. On 26 May 2000 a highlight of the day was a walk across the Sydney Harbour Bridge: an estimated 250,000 people turned out to support the reconciliation process.

Sorry Day was an annual event between 1998 and 2004 and was renamed in 2005 as the National Day of Healing for All Australians.

For Aboriginal people, "sorry business" is the term given broadly to matters of death and mourning. It refers to rituals, feelings and community loss. "Sorry Day" was meant to connote the restoration of hope for indigenous people.

Acknowledgments

I would like to acknowledge that Aboriginal Australians are the traditional custodians of the land about which I write, and that their spiritual and material connection with the land is persistent and precious. This text is written in the hope that further native title grants will be offered in the spirit of reconciliation and in gratitude for all that indigenous Australians have given to others in their country.

The forms of solidarity in writing are many. This novel was completed at two writing residencies, one at the McDowell Artists' Colony in New Hampshire, USA, and the other at the Camargo Foundation at Cassis, in France. I am deeply grateful to both institutions for the provision of a quiet space to write and stimulating fellow residents. Anne McClintock and Alice Attie were both splendid companions, both artists of enormous astuteness, sensitivity and intellectual gifts. Poets Sue Standing, Glorie Simmons and Francis Richards, composer Andrea Clearfield and artist Dore Bowen, all offered specific and interventionist inspiration. Dr. David Green in Boston patiently and lucidly discussed psychiatric issues of child trauma. I am deeply grateful to many supportive friends, particularly Susan Midalia and Victoria Burrows, who both read an early version of this text and offered wonderfully intelligent advice, as did Jane Palfreyman and James Gurbutt. Catherine Hill offered cleverly incisive eleventh-hour editorial commentary, which contributed significantly to the revision of the book. Sue Abbey, whose work I have respected for many years, also contributed clear-sighted and circumspect advice. Thanks, too, to Amanda Nettlebeck, for a timely and illuminating discussion on the ethics of writing, and Hilary Rumley who generously assisted with anthropological information. Both Michelle de Kretser and Elizabeth Smither provided for me the model of utterly wise, poised and dedicated writers; I thank both for our reassuring literary conversations.

I am particularly indebted to Carlos Ferguson, who cautiously, and in a spirit of artistic collaboration, showed me the beauty of sign language at Annamakerig. Thanks to Daniel Brown for his spontaneous generosity in offering me a special space in which to begin my final reading of the text. Professor John Norman kindly shared his detailed memories of Broome in war-time. Any errors, historical or otherwise, are of course mine.

My colleagues at the University of Western Australia have been, once again, magnificently supportive and Zoe Waldie has been a consistently brilliant literary agent.

My family share, or don't share, my own early memories of Broome; in both cases they have been the source of wonderful conversations and the endlessly involving pleasures of nostalgia.

Page 207 cites words inspired by Emily Dickinson's Poem 341 which can be found in ed. Thomas H. Johnson, *Emily Dickinson: The Complete Poems* (London & Boston: Faber and Faber, 1987) p. 162.

The quote on page 156 is drawn from Joseph Conrad, *Heart of Darkness*, ed. Robert Hampson (London: Penguin Classics 2000) p. 87.

Knowledge of the Broome woman spirit mentioned on p. 119 comes from Anne Brewster, Angeline O'Neill and Rosemary van den Berg's book, *Those Who Remain Will Always Remember: An Anthology of Aboriginal Writing* (co-edited, Perth: Fremantle Arts Centre Press, 2000).

The quote from *Rebecca* is reproduced with the permission of the Curtis Brown Group Ltd, London, on behalf of the Estate of Daphne du Maurier and is copyright © Daphne du Maurier.

ABOUT THE AUTHOR

Gail Jones teaches literature, cinema, and cultural studies at the University of Western Australia. Her novel *Dreams of Speaking* was nominated for the Orange Prize in 2006, and her debut novel, *Sixty Lights,* was nominated for the MAN Booker Prize in 2004. She lives in Perth.

Now Available from Europa Editions

A
Amazing Disgrace,
James Hamilton-Paterson

B
Between Two Seas, Carmine Abate
The Big Question, Wolf Erlbruch
Boot Tracks, Mathew F. Jones
Broken Colors, Michele Zackheim
The Butterfly Workshop, Wolf Erlbruch

C
Carte Blanche, Carlo Lucarelli
Chourmo, Jean-Claude Izzo
Cooking with Fernet Branca, James Hamilton-Paterson

D
The Damned Season, Carlo Lucarelli
The Days of Abandonment, Elena Ferrante
Death's Dark Abyss, Massimo Carlotto
Departure Lounge, Chad Taylor
Dog Day, Alicia Giménez-Bartlett

F
Fairy Tale Timpa, Altan
Fresh Fields, Peter Kocan
The Fugitive, Massimo Carlotto

G
The Girl on the Via Flaminia, Alfred Hayes
The Goodbye Kiss, Massimo Carlotto

H
Hangover Square, Patrick Hamilton
The Have-Nots, Katharina Hacker
Here Comes Timpa, Altan

I
I Loved You for Your Voice, Sélim Nassib

J
The Jasmine Isle, Ioanna Karystiani

L
Lions at Lamb House, Edwin M. Yoder Jr.
Little Criminals, Gene Kerrigan
The Lost Daughter, Elena Ferrante
The Lost Sailors, Jean-Claude Izzo
Love Burns, Edna Mazya

M
Margherita Dolce Vita, Stefano Benni
The Midnight Choir, Gene Kerrigan
Minotaur, Benjamin Tammuz
The Miracle of the Bears, Wolf Erlbruch

O
Old Filth, Jane Gardam
One Day a Year, Christa Wolf